NORFOLK LIBRARY
AND INFORMATION SERVICE

RANGE OF TERROR

Pat Harmon, sometime lawman, sometime cowboy, pressed himself against the cliffs in the dark night. He had been a fool to accept the job of ridding the county of an unseen but deadly menace, known as the 'Ghost Dog', which had left a trail of dead and mutilated people. Even now, he wished he could saddle up and ride away, but he couldn't — not if it meant leaving Callie Hebert. Suddenly, tiny sounds break the stillness of the night, and pandemonium erupts . . .

BILLY HALL

RANGE OF
TERROR

Complete and Unabridged

LINFORD
Leicester

First published in Great Britain in 2012 by
Robert Hale Limited
London

First Linford Edition
published 2013
by arrangement with
Robert Hale Limited
London

A catalogue record for this book is available
from the British Library.

ISBN 978–1–4448–1777–5

Published by
F. A. Thorpe (Publishing)
Anstey, Leicestershire

Set by Words & Graphics Ltd.
Anstey, Leicestershire
Printed and bound in Great Britain by
T. J. International Ltd., Padstow, Cornwall

This book is printed on acid-free paper

1

Patrick O'Moynihan sipped the strong coffee, savoring it intensely. 'Sure, Patty boy, and 'tis a fine cup o' coffee you're makin',' he complimented himself. 'I couldn't have made better meself. And the rabbit you shot was roasted to perfection, if I do say so.'

He tossed the last bone, still with most of its meat, to his dog. 'Here you go, Ralph, me boy. The rest of it is all yours.'

The dog grabbed the last of the rabbit out of the air. Patrick leaned back with his cup of coffee and listened to the dog happily chewing on the bone. Life was good. He'd been punching cows for three months for this spread, and he loved it. Other ranches he had worked had been far less enjoyable.

The ONO wouldn't have been all that bad, if it hadn't been for Sandy

Johnson. Sandy seemed to have it in for almost everybody, but especially Irishmen. To make it worse, Oscar Osbeck, the owner, thought Sandy called the moon to rise and set. Or so it seemed to Patrick. That meant that every trumped up thing he told the boss about Patrick was instantly accepted as gospel. Patrick was given the worst of the hated jobs all the time, and constantly threatened with being fired.

The 666 ranch wasn't a good fit for Patrick from the first. He never could understand why one as religious as Walter Finney would pick a brand that was the very mark of the Beast. He said it was to show the devil he had no fear of him, but that made no sense. You didn't choose the devil's brand to defy him. Anyway, because he was Irish, they assumed that Patrick was a Papist, and they rode him constantly about it. He had felt like he had escaped from the Grand Inquisition when he had found a job on a different ranch and drawn his time.

2

The worst of all, though, had been the Mill Iron. Silas McGovern was the hardest boss he had ever heard of. He demanded that his hands be in the saddle when the first rays of the sun gilded the horizon. There was neither rest nor respite until the last rays of that sun were gone, and the crew had to ride back to the ranch in the dark. And it was that way seven days a week, every week of the year. If, by chance, there wasn't enough work, Silas would find work. There wasn't a loose plank or a crooked post in any corral on the place. His buildings were the only ones in the country that were all painted. He had even insisted that they paint the roof of the big horse barn. Cedar shakes, painted that gosh-awful red, just like the rest of the buildings. Except the house, of course, which was white. When Patrick drew his time and left the Mill Iron, he went to town, got a room, and slept for two days before he even started to drink up the paltry wages Silas had paid.

Then he'd gotten the chance to go to work on the LRH. Lester Hebert didn't believe in making his hands work on Sunday, except during calving or weaning times, and sometimes during haying, if the weather had been hindering their laying by enough hay for winter. When the work was slack he had no problem with the boys goofing off, now and then. They could break wild horses they'd caught for their own strings, or to sell. Those that were working toward a place of their own could take part of their pay in cows, and run them with the boss's at no charge, up to a hundred head apiece. And the hands all treated each other like men. They pulled pranks and hurrawed foul-ups and demanded that everybody pull his weight, but they did it without malice. Patrick fit in from the first, and he loved it.

Well, it was that way until that spooky stuff started. But even now, it was a great place to work. He didn't give any weight to that creepy stuff anyway. Just somebody with too big an imagination. Or too many wee nips from a bottle.

Ralph growled suddenly. Patrick rose to his feet and eased back away from his small campfire, out of its circle of light. 'Sure an' what's worryin' you, Ralph?' he asked softly. As if in answer, the dog walked straight away from him. He walked stiff-legged. His tail was straight out behind him. The hair along his back and neck stood up straight. 'Catamount, I'm bettin',' Patrick breathed.

He drew his forty-five and edged away from the fire. He could neither see nor hear anything. The silence was so profound it seemed as if even the night insects had stopped doing whatever insects do. Nothing stirred. There was no slightest breath of breeze. Then he heard it. It was low, guttural, and like no sound Patrick had ever heard. Chills ran the length of his spine.

He listened a long moment, crouched, gun in hand. Then he grinned. He stood up straight. He holstered his gun. 'OK,

5

boys,' he called out. 'Sure an' I'm knowin' that's the sound you was describin' in the bunkhouse. Settin' me up, you was. Now you've come slippin' out here to try to scare the bejaisus outa me, but it ain't workin'. You'd just as well be comin' to the fire an' havin' a cup o' coffee.'

He turned and started back to the fire. Then he heard Ralph. He thought it was Ralph. It sounded like Ralph, just the beginning of a snarl. Then it ended abruptly in a gurgling, gasping noise unlike anything Patrick had ever heard.

Patrick stopped dead in his tracks. He drew the forty-five again. The moon hadn't yet risen. The night was so dark he could scarcely see his hand in front of his face. 'Ralph?' he called softly. 'Ralph, be you all right, fellow?'

There was no response. There was no sound. The chills were back, running up and down his spine. He didn't think the other hands could make Ralph be that quiet. He whistled sharply. 'C'mon Ralph. Come here,' he commanded.

Silence. Cautiously, putting each foot

down with care, he crept in the direction from which he had heard what he thought was his dog. He had moved about twenty yards when his foot encountered something soft. He jerked back, his gun level in front of him. Nothing moved. There was no sound.

He reached his toe out again. He instantly encountered the same thing. Something was lying on the ground, not moving. He nudged it with his foot. It yielded to the pressure, but gave no sound. He crouched down, straining his eyes to see. The smell of blood suddenly assaulted his nostrils. He reached out a hand. His fingers immediately came into contact with warm fur. 'Ralph?' he asked.

He reached farther, feeling the still body stretched on the ground. He slid his hand along the side of the animal to beneath the front leg, feeling for a heartbeat. There was none. He wished the moon would come up, so he could at least see something. His exploring hand worked its way forward. At the dog's throat the fur was sodden and sticky. He lifted his hand to his nose. 'Blood,' he breathed.

A quick exploration with his left hand revealed that the dog's throat had been torn out so viciously that only the hide on the back of the neck was keeping the head connected to the rest of the body. Patrick backed swiftly away from the dog's body. He couldn't imagine what could have ripped the dog's throat out that horribly, so quickly the dog couldn't even bark or yelp. Nothing could sneak up on Ralph like that. He had ears and a nose like no dog Patrick had ever owned.

In the dark he heard that low, guttural growl again. Then he felt, rather than saw, something hovering over him from behind. He whirled. He knew whatever it was had to be an animal. It certainly wasn't some unearthly creature like the bunkhouse stories had insisted. He didn't believe in anything like that. He sure wasn't going to be scared to death. He squeezed the trigger of his forty-five, purely in reflex, as something ripped his throat away. He tried to cry out, but only managed a gurgling gasp as consciousness slid away.

2

The wind was blowing, of course. The wind always blew in Laramie. By Laramie's standards, it wasn't a particularly windy day. Even so, it whistled mournfully in every window. It rattled every loose sign and shutter. It worked ceaselessly to loosen anything else that wasn't already loose. It whipped under the eaves, seeking to rip the lids off every house and shed. It tugged ceaselessly at cedar shakes on the roofs. It rolled an endless procession of tumbleweeds along the dusty street. It never completely stopped. In its quieter moments it seemed to sigh with the resignation of dried-up dreams and parched lives.

Inside the Silver Spring saloon cowboys and sheep-herders, prospectors and soldiers, drifters and merchants valiantly resisted the effects of the moisture-sucking wind by sipping steadily on their beer, on shots of rye, or on whatever rotgut whiskey the Silver Spring had plenty of at the moment. The ladies who smiled hopefully at them, kept up their efforts against the dryness of the wind.

Four men sat at a table near the back of the Silver Spring. Each held a mug of beer. All four sat bunched on the same half of the round table, so they could see the rest of the room and the front door. Only one seemed uninterested in his beer. 'You reckon he's gonna show up?' one of the four asked.

'He'll show,' the one not drinking his beer replied softly.

'What makes you so sure?' another asked.

'Human nature. No man, no matter how calloused he gets, can stand the constant nagging of a guilty conscience. Add to that the knowledge that someone is after him that just keeps on comin' and comin', and don't never stop. After a while he just wants to get it over with and face the music.'

'Even if it means he'll get shot or hung?'

'Yup. Most people that do the kinda stuff Red's done will sooner or later make sure they get caught. They can't help it. There's just something that causes 'em to make dumb mistakes, or just turn around and face it. There's somethin' deep inside that forces 'em to make sure they get punished for what they did.'

'Yeah, maybe. But that don't mean he's gonna just ride into town and say, 'Here I am. Shoot me.''

'No, he'll figure if he takes me out, he'll be free of that nagging voice inside.'

'He's run this long. What makes you think he won't just keep runnin'?'

'He knows that if he don't show up today I'll just keep comin' after him.'

'Yeah, but if you go out to his digs, then you'd be on his turf.'

'Don't matter. He ain't one to put anything off. He knows he's got it to do, facin' me. He'll do it now, rather than wait.'

He knew that to be as certain as his own determination to put an end to his hunt. Red Atkins had left a trail of dead men and violated women in the Indian Nation and Colorado. He had almost caught up with him at Leadville, but Red had managed to quit the country a few days ahead of him.

If he hadn't accepted the job of finding him, of either arresting or killing him, he might have said 'good riddance', and gotten on with his life. But he couldn't do that. He'd accepted the job. He'd accepted some of the money up front, and he'd spent most of that money for lodging, eats and such. When he'd been about to push on past Laramie, he found out, almost by accident, that Red had holed up on a ranch just north and west. He was working as a cowboy, going by the name of Flint Rogers, but the description was too perfect to be anyone but Red. Especially the scar the length of his left cheek, and the missing top of his right ear.

The scar was from an old knife-fight. The missing piece of ear was from Pat's bullet. He had come that close to ending the hunt back in the Indian Nation. He still wasn't sure how Red had managed to slip away that time, but he'd been on his trail ever since. Seven months and counting. It had been a long trail.

When he figured out where Red was he had simply sent a message. 'Pat Harmon says you can come into Laramie to deal with him, or he'll ride out here. Your choice.'

It seemed kind of melodramatic, even as he sent the message. But he knew how it wore on a man to know someone was relentlessly hunting him. He knew, however bold a front Red put up, that he didn't sleep well. He thought having to stew about it and make a decision which way to face his pursuer would unsettle him. That just might give Pat the edge he needed.

He well knew he needed an edge, if he could gain one. Red Atkins was the fastest gun he had ever faced. He had watched him draw against another gunman once. The other man was one of the fastest guns in the country. His gun hadn't even cleared leather when Red's bullet holed his heart.

'How do you know he won't just light a shuck?' one of the men asked Pat.

Pat shrugged. 'He might, but it's not likely. He's been lookin' over his shoulder, knowin' I was back there somewhere, too long. It'll be eatin' him alive. He'll be just as anxious as I am to be done with it. One way or another.'

The fourth member of the party spoke up for the first time. 'It ain't a good day to face him.'

The other three looked at him with raised eyebrows. 'Why not, Hap? One day's as good as another.'

Hap shook his head in vigorous disagreement. 'Oh, no. No, that just ain't so. There's days that's good for one man but not for another. There's some days that ain't good for nobody. This here's a day that's good for Red, but it ain't good for Pat. No sir, Pat. You hadn't oughta go facin' Red today.'

'Now just how did you figure that out?' one of the others demanded.

'I went an' talked to the Chinaman this mornin'.'

'The Chinaman? The one that runs the café?'

'Yup. That's him. Ling Yung something or other. Them Chinese, they know how to tell these things.'

'Is that so? How do they do know stuff we don't know?'

'Their ancestors been studyin' that stuff for years. They got ways o' starin' at the tea leaves in the bottom o' their cup. They cut chickens open an' study their innards. They watch birds — 'specially ravens. All kinds o' stuff like that.'

'And you asked Ling whether it was a good day for Harmon to face Red in a stand-up gunfight?'

Hap nodded enthusiastically. 'Yeah, I did. I paid him four bits to look into it.'

'You paid him four bits to gut a chicken he was gonna cook today anyway?'

Two of the men laughed uneasily, but

16

they watched Hap intently nonetheless. ' 'Tain't whether he was gonna kill it today anyway what matters,' he insisted. 'It's the words he says ahead o' doin' it. Some o' them funny soundin' sing-song Chinese words. An' then he slits the rooster's throat and splits 'im open and spreads his guts out on the table. He runs his fingers over 'em, makin' funny sounds, kinda up in his nose, like. Then he picks up the cup he just drank tea outa, an' studies the leavin's in the bottom o' the cup. Then he looks up at me and shakes his head, an' he says, 'Not good day for lawman. Bad day for lawman mean good day for bad man. Tell lawman he not do good to face the red hair this day.' '

Hap finished the burst of words. It was more words than the other three had heard him say in the past week. When he finished, he seemed to sag and settle into his chair as if all the wind had just gone out of him. His eyes were cast down, his hands wrapped around his beer.

The other two swivelled their eyes to Pat Harmon's face, awaiting his reaction. Pat watched the front door as if he had heard none of it.

Finally one of his companions said, 'Well? What're you gonna do, Pat?'

Pat didn't favor the speaker with so much as a glance. 'Wait for Red,' he said.

'But you heard Hap. The Chinaman says it ain't a good day for you to do that. Them Chinese know these things. They know stuff the rest of us don't.'

'Well, they know how to speak Chinese, anyway,' Pat agreed.

'That ain't what I mean an' you know it! Dang it, Pat! There ain't no sense in you just tryin' to get yourself kilt.'

'You really oughta pay attention, Pat,' the other man agreed. 'Them Orientals do know that kinda stuff.'

Pat finally favored his companions with a long look. A trace of a smile played at the corners of his mouth. 'Ling works like a dog to scratch out a livin' for him and his family. It's the same with every Chinaman I've ever known. If they all know so much, why aren't they all rich and livin' to be a hundred?'

The others looked at one another, each obviously hoping that someone had an answer. None of the three did. Pat reached into his vest pocket and pulled out his watch. He opened the cover and checked the time. 'Well, if he's gonna show me he ain't afraid of me by showin' up right on time, he oughta be just about at the other end o' Main Street right about now.'

He did nothing to betray the tight knot in his stomach as he stood up and moved around the table. He flexed his right hand a couple times, then lifted the Colt forty-five in its holster and let it back down, assuring himself it rode loose and ready. He strode to the door and stepped out onto the board sidewalk.

As if it were scripted, a lone rider was walking his horse slowly toward him, three blocks away. As if spirited along by some unheard whisper, awareness of the outlaw's presence telegraphed itself along the street. People moving about their business stopped in mid-stride, looked up the street, looked back at Pat, then began to edge off to the sides of the dusty thoroughfare. By the time Pat walked to the middle of the street, nobody stood between him and the horseman.

A hundred yards from Pat, the horseman turned his horse toward the sidewalk. He stepped from the saddle and dropped the reins across a hitchrail. He didn't bother to loop them around it. The horse stood as if securely tethered. The horseman stripped gloves from his hands, and tucked them in his belt. He removed his hat, ran a hand through his rust-colored hair, and put the hat back on. He lifted his revolver from its holster and let it settle back. Then he walked to the center of the street and began to stride purposefully toward Pat. Pat stood where he was, waiting.

Thirty feet away, he stopped. 'You

don't give up easy, do you, Harmon?'

'When I got a job to do, I see it through,' Pat responded.

'I wish you didn't.'

'Me too, sometimes.'

'One of us ain't gonna walk away today.'

'Yeah. Maybe neither one of us. Maybe we'll be like the gingham dog and the calico cat.'

Red actually chuckled. 'We ain't likely to eat each other up. We just might shoot each other, though.'

'It's been known to happen, I've heard.'

'Why're you so dead set on runnin' me down?'

'My job.'

'I figured that out, but who hired you to track me down?'

'The family of that tow-headed kid you killed in the Indian Nation.'

Red nodded, as if he either knew or suspected. 'I did think he had a gun.'

'He didn't.'

'Yeah. I know.'

'Even if he had, you knew he'da been no match for you.'

'There ain't many that are. None, so far.'

'He was only fifteen.'

'That right? He looked older.'

'He was their only kid.'

'Yeah, well, I'll tell you . . . '

Hoping to catch Pat waiting for the rest of the sentence, he whipped his gun from its holster in a blur of motion. It lifted and centered on Pat's chest. At the same instant it reached that point, a chunk of lead tore through Red's sternum, passed through his lungs, and slammed like a sledge-hammer into his spine.

The force of the impact drove him backward. The motion jerked the barrel of Red's gun up at the same instant the hammer dropped. Fire and lead spewed out the end of the barrel. The bullet jerked at the collar of Pat's shirt, singeing a welt across his shoulder at the base of his neck as it passed.

Pat's second shot, instantly behind

the first, blew Red's heart apart and drove him backward and to the ground. He sprawled in the dust of the street, his eyes staring unblinkingly upward at the noon sun.

Pat stood where he was, staring at the dead outlaw. He took in a deep, ragged breath. 'I really wasn't a bit sure I could take him,' he almost whispered.

He was suddenly overwhelmed by an unexpected sense of emptiness. He was, in an instant, a man without a purpose, a destination, or a plan. For more than half a year his whole life had been devoted to pursuing this one man. Now, in one heart-stopping instant, it was over. The sense of loss overwhelmed any sense of satisfaction. The feeling caught him completely off guard. He slowly ejected the spent cartridges from his Colt and replaced them with fresh ones. He reholstered the gun.

The sudden eruption of excited conversations along the street seemed faint and far away. Some part of his mind noticed Heck Thedford, the Laramie County sheriff, heading toward him. Heck bent over and picked Red's gun up out of the dust. He walked over in front of Pat. His pale-blue eyes bore no expression as he reached up and stuck a finger through the hole in the collar of Pat's shirt. 'That's about as close as a man can get to not havin' it matter whether he won or lost.'

'Yeah,' Pat said. 'It stings some. Is it bleedin'?'

'Nope. Red streak. Looks more like a burn than a gunshot wound. Couldn'ta got no closer without drawin' blood. Sorta holed your new shirt, though.'

'Better the shirt than me.'

'I wasn't sure you was right about Flint Rogers really bein' Red Atkins. I figured I'd know if he showed up today to face you.'

'That's why I did it that way. I wanted to be sure I had the right man.'

'You'll be ridin' on, now, I reckon?'

'Yeah.'

'I could use a good deputy.'

'Thanks. There's gotta be a better way to make a livin'.'

'Probably. There's worse ways, too.'

'Yeah.'

'You'll be ridin' on, now, then?'

'I'll be waitin' a few days. I'll wire the folks that hired me, that the job's done. Then I'll have to wait till they get the rest of my money to me.'

'You reckon they will?'

'I reckon.'

Heck nodded. 'I'll have Stilt take care o' buryin' Red, and send his horse back home.'

'Much obliged.'

There didn't seem much else to say.

3

Smoke drifted lazily upward into the twilight sky. The sounds of a fiddle and a squeezebox, accompanied by the rhythmic clapping of dozens of hands, were filling the evening with sounds of 'My Darling Clementine', 'The Big Rock Candy Mountain',' and 'Beulah Land'. The caravan was nearing the end of its intended journey. Relief, thanksgiving and joy bubbled palpably.

The scent of roasted meat, fresh biscuits and a nondescript mixture of spices still hung in the still air. The hunters had done well. All were well fed.

Seventeen covered wagons were arranged in a circle. At nearly every wagon a small fire, or the still smoking remnants of one, gave evidence of the evening meal. In the center of the circle a larger fire blazed. Near it the musicians plied their instruments. People sang along. A few danced in the open space, some of them surprisingly well.

Around the outside of the circle of wagons several guards paced. They kept their backs to the wagons, lest the light of the fires hamper their night vision. They walked the area they were assigned, watching, listening, alert for the encroachment of either man or animal that might mean them harm.

To the west of the wagons the horses and cattle were herded by still others. Most of the cattle were lying down now, contentedly chewing their cuds. They had swiftly filled their bellies with the lush grass that grew along the stream and in the hollows. The horses, as always, just kept on eating.

At the east side of the circled wagons a young man and woman crouched between wagons, holding hands, watching. They watched the pacing sentries, timing when they could slip between them unseen. He squeezed her hand in a wordless signal. Together they ran on silent feet. When he squeezed her hand

27

again, she dropped with him into the tall grass. They had timed the paces of the sentry, so they knew when they had to drop out of sight.

When the right amount of time had elapsed, he rose silently to his feet. Like a shadow she rose with him, and they ran again. This time they were behind a clump of screening bushes before the sentry would have turned. He turned toward her. She came into his arms eagerly. Their lips met and clung together in a long and passionate embrace. He whispered softly, 'Let's move off a ways farther, so we can talk without 'em hearin' us.'

Hand in hand they moved another hundred yards from the wagons. A swale hid them from all sight of the wagons. The music and laughter were so distant they had to strain to hear them. 'Oh, Anton,' the girl said. 'I love you so much!'

'I love you too, Ida Lee. I just can't hardly wait for night to come so we can get a chance to sneak away together.'

'Why don't you just ask my pa to let us get married?' she asked.

' 'Cause he'd say 'No'.'

'He might not.'

'He would. He ain't gonna let us even talk about gettin' married till I at least got a homestead claim filed some-where's. Just as soon as we get where we're goin', I will. I'll get a cabin built, and a shed and corral, then I'll ask him.'

'But that's so long! I can't wait that long, Anton.'

He held her close, his hands caress-ing up and down her body as they kissed again. Then he said, 'We ain't been exactly waitin', have we?'

She giggled. 'We haven't been waiting for anything,' she admitted, 'but I hate having to sneak out every night just so we can make love. I want to be able to sleep in your arms after, instead of having to hurry up and get my hair smoothed and my clothes straightened out, and then sneak back in between the guards.'

'Do you think the guards really don't never see us?'

She jerked as if he had hit her. 'What do you mean?'

He kissed her again, then spoke softly into her ear. 'If it's as easy as it seems for us to sneak out and back in, don't you think Indians would've slipped into the circle and kilt us all a long time ago?'

It was obviously a new thought to her. 'I hadn't thought about that. It's always seemed so easy.'

'Of course it has. They don't wanta catch us. They know what we're doin'.'

The thought obviously terrified her. 'You mean they know we're . . . that . . .'

He laughed softly. 'Well, they don't exactly know all we been doin', but they sure know we been sneakin' out by ourselves every night. I'd bet my watch on it. Them guys that stand guard has been in battles with the Indians and with rustlers and bad guys afore. They ain't dumb.'

'Do you think they've told Ma and Pa?'

He thought about it for a long

moment, then shook his head in the darkness. 'I doubt it. They'll keep it to theirselves. They likely figure we're just waitin' till we get where we're goin' to get married anyway. We ain't made no secret o' plannin' that. So they just look the other way an' keep their mouths shut.'

As he talked he kept trying to unbutton her bodice, but she kept pushing his hands away. 'What's wrong? You ain't feelin' romantic tonight?'

She just held on to his hands for a long moment. 'It . . . I . . . it don't seem right, doing that out here in the dark with them knowing what we're doing.'

'That hasn't bothered you up to now,' he teased.

He caught the glint of moonlight on a tear sliding down her cheek. He frowned. He reached out a hand and wiped it away. 'What's the matter, Ida Lee? What are you cryin' for?'

She shook her head as if trying to sort out her thoughts. 'I just don't want folks thinking I'm some kinda tramp. If

31

the guards know we're sneaking off, then everyone's going to just assume that's what we're doing, and my reputation will be ruined. Anton, I don't think we ought to do this any more. Not until we get where we're going and get married, and can do it right and honest.'

'You mean just quit doin' it?'

'We managed to do without it before we started.'

'Yeah, but we did start. I don't know if I can do without now.'

'I guess you'll have to. I'm not going to sneak out with you any more.'

'For real?'

'For real.'

'But I love you!'

'I love you too, Anton. I love you more than anything in the whole world. But I want other folks to respect both of us, too. So we're just going to stop doing what we been doing until we can get married.'

He stiffened suddenly. 'What's wrong?' she whispered, suddenly alarmed.

He whispered back, 'I don't know. I

thought I heard something.'

'From the wagons?'

'No. From over there.'

He turned and pointed straight away from the wagons. She stepped a little bit to one side to see if she could see something. Suddenly something hurtled out of the night, slamming into both of them simultaneously. They both opened their mouths to cry out, to scream. Unbearable pressure clamped both of their throats closed before any sound could escape. Indescribable pain rocketed through them both as the pressure left, taking veins and arteries, breath and life, along with it. Neither was able to do more than make a choked, gurgling gasp. The pain subsided almost at once. So did all other sensation. They never even felt the long, soft grass that screened their bodies from the rising moon.

At the east edge of the wagon train a guard stopped in his pacing. He lifted his gun and cocked his head to one side, listening intently. A dozen yards to his side another guard noticed the change instantly. 'What?' he whispered.

'Thought I heard somethin'.'

'What'd you hear, Jim?'

'Not sure. Somethin'.'

'Want me to tell Cap?'

'Yeah. Ask him for Kit, Lonnie an' Joe. We'll check it out.'

With no further sound, the second guard disappeared. Moments later three men materialized beside Jim. He motioned silently. The four spread out into an evenly spaced line. Crouching and walking silently on moccasins, they crept forward.

At the clump of bushes they separated, rounding it silently and warily from both sides. In the moonlight the pair's trail in the tall grass was as clear to them as a worn roadway. They spread out again, following that trail, watching, listening.

As they topped the rim of the swale in which the lovers had sought shelter, they stopped. Though they could not see the bodies, they sensed where they were. They didn't know whether the couple were trying to hide, or were dead. They stood stock still for several minutes. When there was no sound or motion from the couple, they crept forward. As they neared, first one, then the others jerked their heads up. They could not mistake the musky smell of fresh blood. They knew with certainty what they were about to find. They afforded the dead duo one quick glance. That was adequate to be sure they were dead. That was also adequate to know it was something they had never encountered that had killed the two.

No Indians killed like that. If it were Indians, they would have had their heads caved in with tomahawks, or their throats slashed, not ripped out raggedly, with everything from chin to chest completely gone. If it were a catamount or wolves, the animals would have immediately begun to feast on the warm flesh. The four, expert trackers all, moved as one toward the other side of the swale. They could see where something — two somethings — had come over the lip of the swale, then leaped, or flown, the last twenty feet to where they slammed into the hapless couple.

Whatever it was had left just as quickly. It hadn't bothered to tear at the bodies. It hadn't eaten any part of them. It had simply torn their throats out and left, all in near total silence. They were able to track whatever it was in the tall grass until they came to a stretch of ground that bore little vegetation. The hard ground left no trace of whatever had passed over it. They fanned out and searched as best they could in the moonlight, but it seemed as if whatever had attacked had simply disappeared into thin air. 'We gotta get Cap,' Jim said needlessly.

'We can't just leave them two lyin' there while we do,' Kit fretted.

'They're already dead,' Lonnie argued. 'We'd best stay together, an' make sure nobody moves in anything less than groups o' four comin' back after 'em.'

They moved in a silent, furtive cluster, watching, listening in all directions until they were back at the wagons. Cap immediately tripled the guard, and sent a party of eight men to retrieve the bodies. Then they settled down to wait in a mixture of grief and terror for the sun to come up. What they found when the sun finally favored them with its light shed no more illumination on what had happened than the moon had shown. Whatever attacked and killed the young lovers had vanished with no trace beyond that few yards at the swale.

The wagon train buried their dead and moved on. They stopped to grieve, restock their supplies, and share their terror at the town of Prosper Gulch. It did not provide any consolation to them to discover that the victims from their group were not the first. It did provide certainty that they would neither stop nor settle anywhere close to that area.

4

Pat Harmon leaned against the post that supported the porch roof. He fished a bag of Bull Durham out of his shirt pocket, along with the sheaf of cigarette papers. He opened the sheaf of papers and blew gently on the edge, lifting the single sheet that the breath separated from the rest. He slid the rest of the sheaf of papers back in his pocket. Making a trough of the single paper with a thumb and two fingers, he carefully shook a quantity of tobacco from the bag along the paper trough. He flipped the bag of tobacco so the tag on the end of the string loop that surrounded the top swung upward. He caught the tag with his lips and pulled, so the drawstring drew the bag tightly closed. He replaced the bag of tobacco in his pocket. With the index finger of his now free hand, he evened out the tobacco in the paper trough, then rolled the paper around it. He ran his tongue along the edge of the paper and sealed it closed around the tobacco. He twisted one end of the paper closed, then put the other end in his mouth.

Watching the activity along the main street of Laramie, he fished in his pants pocket for a match. Having extracted one, he raised one foot so that his trouser leg was stretched tightly along the underside of his thigh. He raked the match swiftly along the coarse cloth, and the match flared. He touched the match to the twisted end of the cigarette as he drew the smoke through the tobacco. He drew it deeply into his lungs as he whipped out the match and dropped it in the street. He stood there enjoying the smoke as he studied the street scene he no longer saw. Instead he was trying his best to see his own future. For the first time that he could remember, he was completely foot-loose, with no plans, no job, no prospects.

He had collected the rest of the money due to him for bringing the killer of the young boy in the Indian Nation to justice. The death of Red Atkins had been deeply satisfying, but deeply depressing at the same time. He had been a man who badly needed to be shot or hung. He had left a trail of death and atrocities across 500 miles of the West. The world was certainly better off without him.

On the other hand, Pat had spent the better part of a year in pursuit of the man. It had become the whole reason for his own existence. Now that reason was gone, and he felt empty, hollow, completely at loose ends. He supposed other men would take advantage of the sizable chunk of money he now had to go on a long spree of drunken carousing. The ladies at the Silver Spring, or any of Laramie's other establishments, would gladly assist him in getting rid of the money. That whole idea simply held no great appeal for Pat. He craved the company of a woman, to be sure, but not one he had to pay to pretend she couldn't resist his charms.

Heck had offered him a job as a deputy, but that consisted mostly of rousting drunken cowboys and such from the saloons, dragging them to the jail to sleep off the night's drink, then turning them loose in the morning with a headache and whatever festering 'souvenir' they had picked up from that saloon's 'ladies' the night before. That kind of job simply didn't appeal to him. So what was he going to do? He dropped the stub of the cigarette into the street and stepped on it to extinguish it. He ambled down the street to the Silver Spring saloon.

He paused inside the door to let his eyes adjust. He had struck up a friendship with three hands from an area ranch, who were in town drinking up the past few months' wages and making the acquaintance of as many of the saloon's 'ladies' as they could. They were a friendly trio and he enjoyed their company. To a point. He spotted them

41

at once, seated at the table they had been holding down for the past week. He crossed the sawdust-covered floor and took a seat facing the front door.

'Howdy, Pat,' the trio said at almost the same time.

'Hap, Slim, Butch,' Pat responded. 'You boys stayin' sober today?'

'Just sober enough to know whether I'm havin' a good time,' Slim responded.

'I didn't save up four months' wages, then come to town to stay sober,' Butch chimed in.

'I'm gonna stay sober enough to know better'n to take Matilda upstairs again,' Hap said. 'That is one nasty whore.'

'Rough, is she?'

'Not rough. Just dirty. She stinks worse'n Bathless Baker. Got a mouth on her, too. I don't like a woman talkin' like that. It ain't seemly.'

'But bein' a whore is?'

Hap seemed at a loss for an answer, so he just sipped his beer instead.

'You boys had lunch?' Pat asked.

'Not yet. We was fixin' to holler at

Dub to bring us a sandwich. He makes a good beef sandwich, and he always puts a good bait o' beans on the plate. Two bits for all you wanta eat.'

'Sounds good. I'll buy you boys lunch today.'

'You get your money?'

'Yup.'

Butch turned toward the bar and called out to Dub. When the bartender looked at him, he said, 'You wanta feed us four hungry souls?'

'What I got ain't gonna do your souls a bit o' good,' Dub retorted, 'but I'll whip up somethin' to fill your bellies.'

'We'll settle for that,' Butch grinned.

He turned back to Pat. 'So what're you gonna do now?'

Pat's eyes clouded. He shrugged. 'Don't rightly know. I may drift on up north a ways toward the mountains. Look around. See what jumps out at me.'

'Mountain lion or a grizzly, most likely,' Hap said. 'I don't much like the mountains.'

'I always thought I'd like to ride for

43

an outfit on the edge of the mountains,' Slim countered. 'A man could be in the high country in the summer, then down where the winters is bearable the rest o' the year.'

They chatted about the relative merits of ranching in different environs until Dub came over with four plates. Each held a thick sandwich, with generous amounts of roast beef between thick slices of buttered bread. Each plate had an equally generous amount of steaming beans.

'Dub makes a fine pot o' beans,' Butch commented.

Slim stood abruptly. He whipped his hat off and placed it over his heart. He began to speak, as if reciting something of great and melodramatic importance.

Beans, beans, that musical fruit,
The more you eat, the more you
    toot,
The more you toot, the better you
    feel.
Oh, what a wonderful, musical meal.

'Sit down and shut up,' Butch ordered. 'You sound like a Sky Pilot.'

'Downright poetical,' Pat disagreed. 'Where'd you learn that?'

Before Slim could respond, Butch hollered at Dub. 'Hey, Dub. Could we have some salt?'

Without answering, Dub came around the end of the bar with a salt shaker and placed it in the center of their table. He'd no sooner set it down than Slim reached across his plate, picked up his beer to wash down a bite of his sandwich, and knocked over the salt shaker. A small amount of salt spilled out onto the table.

'Dang!' Hap said instantly, springing to his feet.

Before the others could even figure out what the problem was, Hap shoved things aside to make a clear path between the spilled salt and the edge of the table. He took his hand and carefully brushed every grain of the salt to the edge of the table, then off the edge into the cupped palm of his other hand. He sat back down, muttered something, and tossed the retrieved salt over his left shoulder.

Slim and Butch went on eating their lunch, ignoring him. Pat stared at him in confusion. 'What's that all about?' he asked.

Hap looked at him as if he were some strange sort of creature. 'You don't know what bad luck that is, to spill salt?'

Pat shook his head. 'Bad luck?'

'The worst! Terrible things'll happen, if you go spillin' salt.'

'Never heard such a thing.'

'It's true, I'm tellin' you! The only thing that'll keep it from bein' a disaster is if you manage to brush it up and toss it over your left shoulder. Gotta be the left one. Gotta be sittin' down when you do it, just like you was when it got spilt. Gotta be sure you get all of it. That'll maybe head off the bad luck, but that's the only thing that will.'

Between bites, Butch said, 'Hap's real superstitious about such things.'

'All sorts o' things,' Slim agreed. 'I

seen him turn around and ride all the way around a town once and come in from the other way, just 'cause a black cat walked across the road in front of us.'

'We was sittin' in the hotel lobby one day,' Butch chimed in, 'and some guy was sittin' in a chair readin' a newspaper. He had one foot stuck out, and was rockin' a rockin'-chair that was next to him. Hap went over an' pertneart clobbered the guy for rockin' that empty chair.'

'What harm does that do?' Pat queried.

'Are you kiddin'?' Hap exclaimed. 'That's even worse than puttin' your hat on the bed. You rock an empty chair, it means somebody close to you's gonna die. Just like puttin' your hat on a bed, only then it'll be someone real close to you, like someone that shares your bed. Or you, if it's just your own bed.'

Pat took a big bite of his sandwich, and pondered Hap's predictions until his mouth was empty. Then he said, 'So

47

just exactly how does that work? What is there about those things that causes bad luck?'

Hap shrugged. 'I don't know that anybody knows. It just does. There's realms we can't see in this world, and what we do affects 'em. It plumb behooves us to know what things affect 'em, and see to it we don't go rilin' 'em up.'

'Like the other day being a bad day for me to go up against Red?' Pat reminded him.

Slim and Butch both laughed. Hap turned red. 'It was just plumb foolish, even if you did come out on top. It was a near thing. He didn't miss you by more'n an inch or two.'

'But he missed me.'

Hap struggled for an answer, then settled for attacking his sandwich. Butch said, 'Me'n Slim don't hold to that stuff, but Hap sure does.'

'I guess I don't either,' Pat opined. 'Seems like nonsense to me.'

The weeks to come would challenge that in ways he couldn't have imagined.

48

5

'I ain't takin' no more chances. We're pullin' out.'

Art Hoover rubbed the back of his neck and head thoughtfully. 'That don't make sense, Will. You'n Winnie got your homestead half proved up. You got a snug house. Decent shed for the milk cows and horses. You've put a lot o' work into that place. You got them two young'uns. It's the only home they've known.'

Will Lindstraton nodded his head in agreement with everything Art said, but he was unmoved. 'I know all that, Art. And I know we're owin' you a bit o' money for supplies, too. And we'll get the money back to you. We're good for it.'

'It ain't the money I'm worried about, Will. It's you folks. What're you gonna do? Where you gonna go?'

Will looked back over his shoulder at the makeshift covered wagon. Within it was stacked everything they owned in the world. Two milk cows were tethered to the back of the wagon. A four-year-old boy and a five-year-old girl each rode a horse, close beside the wagon. Wilfred and Winifred sat side by side on the seat. A nice team of Belgians was hitched to the wagon. 'I don't know,' Will admitted. 'I figure we'll be able to catch up to that wagon train that came through two days ago. Maybe we'll throw in with them, settle where they do.'

'I think they were planning to settle around here, till they lost the young folks.'

Will nodded vigorously. 'That's exactly what I mean. The way they lost them two, I mean. Right next to the wagons, practically, with guards posted and even knowin' where they was sneakin' off to, together, like kids do, now and again. When somethin' can appear outa nowheres like that, and rip their throats out that-away, an' not even make a sound enough for the guards to hear — why, that just ain't natural. That ain't rightly possible, only it happened. An' not just to them. Look how many it's happened to. This here part o' the country is cursed. It's gotta be demons, that's what it is. An' I ain't gonna get my family killed on accounta some curse. We're cuttin' out while we're all still alive to do it.'

Art opened his mouth twice to respond, but couldn't think of anything to say. He looked around them at the street in Prosper Gulch. Every man in sight either carried a rifle or shotgun, or wore a pistol. Nearly half the women on the street wore a revolver. He had never seen everybody so frightened, so jumpy. By sundown he knew every person in town would be ensconced in their homes with the doors locked and barricaded. Shades and curtains would be pulled. Everybody in the house would be within reach of a gun, even while they slept.

Even the saloons were suffering a lack of business. Those in the saloons left by dark. Only the saloon on the first floor of the hotel had any business after dark. Their customers could go to their rooms without venturing outside. The whores in the other saloons offered their customers the privilege of sharing their bed for the night. The rest of the saloon's patrons who stayed too late slept off their drink slumped over a table, afraid to step outside.

The words 'siege mentality' ran through Art's mind. That summed it up. The whole area was under siege. It was under siege from something nobody had seen or heard and survived. If something wasn't done, the whole country was going to be deserted. But what could anybody do against something that had to be a specter or a demon? Whatever it was, it was deadly. And it was terrifying people who were normally afraid of nothing. Finally he simply said, 'Well, I'm sorry to see you folks go, but I understand. Don't worry about what you owe me. I'll just write it off.'

'We'll get it to you,' Will promised.

Art knew he would, if he could. If he and his family survived, and got out of the country in one piece. They weren't the first to pull stakes. He knew with glum certainty that they wouldn't be the last.

6

The cat was ugly. In fact, it was beyond ugly. To say that cat was ugly was like saying a tornado was a bit breezy. It was a big tom cat, really big for a cat. One ear had long since been ripped half off in a fight with something. The remainder of the ear lopped over to one side. When he perked up his ears, the half-ear perked up, and the other ear flopped to a different angle.

Another confrontation at some time in the past had left a scar across its face that passed across its eye. That the eyelid still functioned was a wonder. It didn't open entirely. When the eye was closed, the scar looked gruesomely out of place. When the eye was as far open as it would go, it looked like the top half of the eye was covered with a lump of scar tissue that resembled a huge wart.

Its hide was scarred and patchy.

Blotches of hair tufted outward around and along nearly hairless parts of its hide. Most of the hairless lines and patches were scar tissue. Those blotches of hair that ringed the scars all seemed longer than its other fur, standing out in protrusions of disorderly spikes. Its tail was three inches shorter than it should have been. The last two or three inches of remaining tail flopped around randomly, and didn't function with the rest of its tail. Whatever the rest of the tail did, the end seemed to rebel against.

Its disposition was even uglier than its appearance. It ignored any and all people who attempted to approach it, so long as they kept their distance. If they became insistent, however, or simply came too close, he would issue one growl of warning. If that warning wasn't instantly heeded, he would attack with a ferocity that would have shamed a Tasmanian Devil. Even if someone inadvertently approached too close, he was likely to launch a full-blown attack, biting, snarling and clawing, then scurrying away before whatever he had attacked could react.

Every dog on the ranch lived in mortal fear of that unearthly specimen of unpredictable feline fury. If he approached while they were eating something, he had only to growl and the dogs would slink away. They wouldn't return to their interrupted meal until the cat had eaten what he wanted and left.

Even the horses gave him a wide berth. So also did the cowboys. All of them, that is, except Clyde. The cat might have belonged to Clyde Upton. It seemed more likely that Clyde belonged to the cat. At least, he was the one the cat adopted when it straggled into the LRH ranch yard, half dead from starvation and festering wounds of battle. It had simply walked up to Clyde, sat down in front of him, and meowed once. It wasn't a plaintive meow. It sounded more like a command.

Clyde had nursed the bedraggled

creature back to health, and it was his. In his typical twist of irony, Clyde had named the ill-natured beast 'Sweetie Pie'. He kept the unseemly creature alive, in more ways than one. Clyde was well past his prime, but his reputation caused even the young and rowdy among the cowboys to walk softly around him. Clyde let it be known that the cat belonged to him, and anyone who harmed it would deal with him. It was solely for that reason that one or another of the hands hadn't long since used him for target practice. It was hinted around the bunkhouse that one or more well-clawed cowboys had offered a reward for anyone who would do the deed, but so far there had been no takers.

From the day the cat had sufficiently recuperated, it had been Clyde's constant companion. Clyde's string of horses were the only ones on the ranch that were not afraid of Sweetie Pie. The rest avoided him warily. In fact, everyone on the ranch believed that any other horse than those in Clyde's string would have run straight into the jaws of a mountain lion to get away from him. Clyde's horses, on the other hand, simply ignored him, or reached a nose down to him as he passed by. In those instances Sweetie Pie usually just ignored the horse.

Whenever Clyde rode out of the yard, Sweetie Pie accompanied him. Most of the time he ran alongside. At times, however, for reasons nobody knew, he would choose to ride. Whenever he did, he would leap onto Clyde's boot that was in the stirrup, then up to the back of the saddle. He would settle down on top of Clyde's bedroll and ride as if it were his horse that he merely allowed Clyde to share.

He always rode facing backward. If he lay down, it was across the bedroll, facing back the way they had come. If he sat up, he sat straight and tall, still watching their back-trail, as if that were his assigned duty. Thus it was that Clyde and Sweetie Pie rode out together to check the cows that should have been grazing in the vicinity of Thistle Creek.

'I'll be needin' four of you boys to ride up along Thistle Crick and check on them three-year-olds,' Les Hebert had announced at breakfast.

Silence snapped a lid down onto the long table like the bar of a mouse trap. In its wake, it seemed as if nobody dared even breathe. Eyes around the table darted back and forth, each with obvious fear that his name was about to be announced.

Clyde Upton broke the strained silence. 'No need for that, Les,' he drawled. 'Me'n Sweetie Pie'll check 'em out.'

Lester shook his head. 'There ain't no way I'm sendin' just one man. It's too far up there and back to make it in one day, and be back before dark. I'll send four of you, so you can all keep an eye out. When you sack out for the night, keep two awake and watchin' while the other two sleep, and don't step outa each other's sight at night.'

The fearful silence settled back as if it owned the table and its occupants. Clyde shook his head. 'Me'n Sweetie Pie can handle it, boss,' he drawled again. 'Sweetie Pie can see in the dark better'n any critter out there. We'll be fine.'

Clyde turned his attention back to the hunk of steak and the fried potatoes on his plate, as if the matter were settled. Lester appeared about to argue. He looked around the table. Every face that peered back betrayed its owner's hope that he would accept the grizzled veteran's offer. Finally he shrugged. 'Well, if that's the way you want it, it's you for it,' he surrendered. 'But if one of you gets killed up there, you make sure it's that ugly cat.'

Strangely, nobody laughed. Instead, silence commanded the scene again. Hurriedly, Lester rattled off the duties for the crew for the day, then retreated to the ranch house. Several of the riders stopped by Clyde as he tied his bedroll onto his saddle and filled the saddle-bags with whatever he thought he might need. They each in turn offered to accompany him, brave in their certainty that their offers would be refused. They all were.

His horse's ground-eating trot bore him and Sweetie Pie to Thistle Creek by mid-afternoon. Sweetie Pie had run alongside during the morning. They stopped at a seep spring about midday. Clyde shared his lunch with Sweetie Pie while the horse drank and grazed. When they left there, Sweetie Pie jumped up onto the saddle, taking ownership of his post on top of the bedroll.

The herd that was spread out along a mile of Thistle Creek were in top condition. Clyde kept count of cows and calves, jotting the numbers and locations down in the tally book such as every cowboy carried for exactly that duty. He roped two half-grown calves and doctored problems he had spotted.

He roped one cow by both front feet. She had a big clump of brush tangled in her tail, forcing her to drag it around behind her, helpless to use her tail to

61

swish away the ever-present flies. His horse kept the rope taut, keeping her from regaining her feet as she bellowed furiously at the indignity and helplessness. He used his knife to cut away the tangled hairs of her tail and free the brush. When he finished, he remounted, released the tension of the rope, and let her shake the loop from her front feet. As he expected, as soon as she regained her feet, she charged him. His horse easily evaded the enraged bovine's attack. He trotted away, leaving her to bawl her outrage and ingratitude. He saw no hint of problems anywhere. The whole valley along Thistle Creek seemed almost idyllic.

He camped in a copse of aspen trees beside a spring that fed into the creek. Over a small fire he cooked his supper and made coffee. With his stomach full, he cradled the last cup of coffee in both hands. He contentedly sipped its contents as he watched the glorious hues of the sunset fade into the darkness of night.

When he finished the coffee, he rolled into his bedroll and was asleep in minutes. What woke him three hours later he never knew. He had survived a lot of years by never questioning his instincts. Wide awake instantly, he slid from his blankets, gun in hand. Not knowing why, his attention was fixed on a point south and west of his camp. He stood silently with his back against a big aspen tree and waited.

Abruptly a harsh snarl erupted a hundred yards straight in front of him. It was followed instantly by something that sounded almost like a yelp of surprise. Then the sounds of a pitched battle between two or more animals brought the darkness alive with snarls, growls, roars and howls. As suddenly as it started, the noise stopped. Utter silence replaced it. Even the normal night sounds of scurrying animals and insects seemed stilled.

Clyde stood motionless, gun in hand, peering into the darkness, turning his head only as far as necessary to see out to the sides. His heart hammered, but he appeared to be cast in stone, except for the darting of his eyes and the occasional turning of his head.

Fifteen minutes later Sweetie Pie sauntered out of the darkness. Clyde's breath exhaled explosively. He holstered his gun and knelt down, confident there was nothing that now threatened. 'What's goin' on, Sweetie Pie?'

The cat sat down in front of him and stared inscrutably at him. Clyde examined him carefully in the moonlight. His fur was more disheveled than normal. His feet were bloody, but none of it appeared to be his. 'Clawed somethin' purty good, didn't ya?' Clyde commented.

Sweetie Pie began to groom himself as if he had just dispatched a pesky cur that had dared to invade his territory. Then Clyde noticed the blood on his shoulder. 'Whatd'ya have here, Sweetie Pie?' he queried.

Examining the shoulder carefully, he determined that the wound was minor. Turning to his saddle-bags, he extracted a container of ointment and smeared it generously on the wound that had already stopped bleeding. 'Somethin' pertnear got a hunk of you, boy,' he said.

The cat disdained to respond. Instead he stretched prodigiously, marched over to Clyde's bedroll and curled up to sleep. Taking his cue from the cat, Clyde climbed back into his blankets and nearly beat the cat to sleep.

7

'You boys had best just stay home for now.'

'But, Pa! You promised us we could go campin' up by Wilson Falls!'

Art Hoover made no effort to mask the fear in his eyes. 'I know I did, boys. But that was way last winter, when none of this killin' had started. It's just too dangerous now.'

'Not where we're goin',' Isaiah argued. 'Wilson Falls is way up in the foothills. It's pertneart up to the big mountains. There ain't been nothin' happenin' up there. It's all been down around Thistle Crick and around that area.'

'But you have to go through that area to get to where you're wantin' to go,' Art pointed out.

The quieter, more thoughtful voice of the older of Art's two boys entered the discussion for the first time. 'I think Ike's right, Pa,' Josiah said. 'I'll admit we'll be close to where some of the killin's have taken place, but we'll go on through there in daylight. Nothin's happened anywhere in daylight. It's all in the middle of the night, sometime. By nightfall we'll be clear past where anything's happened. And you did promise.'

'It just isn't worth the risk,' Art insisted.

'Joe's right, Pa. You did promise. Besides, there ain't nothin' that doesn't have some risk. If we always just do what's safe, we ain't never goin' to do nothin'. You opened up a store here in Prosper Gulch when everybody said you was crazy and you'd lose everything you'd worked for your whole life. But you took the risk anyway. And you was right.'

'There's a difference between risking money and risking lives.'

'Not really,' Josiah argued. 'Risk is risk. We just have to weigh the risk against the possible gain, and not let a reasonable risk dictate what we do.'

'There is no real gain from this camping trip,' Art argued. 'It's just an adventure. A lark. You're not going to be any less for it, if you decide not to go.'

'Yes we will!' Isaiah interjected instantly. 'We'll be labeled yellow-bellied sissies by everyone that knows us. We been tellin' everyone all winter and spring how we was goin' to do this campin' trip. If we chicken out now, we'll be labeled cowards our whole lives.'

'You'll be labeled as sensible,' Art disputed.

'It doesn't work that way, Pa,' Josiah replied in his infuriatingly calm, reasoned voice. 'Once the other kids find out we didn't go because we were afraid of what might happen, we won't be able to hold our heads up at school or anywhere else. I'd rather die than be labeled a coward. But that's not the point. The point is, there isn't any real danger where we'll be going.'

'Besides, we're reg'lar mountain men, Pa,' Isaiah enthused. 'Me'n Joe can slip through the timber quieter'n a whisper. An' there ain't nothin' that moves within three hundred yards that we don't both notice straight away. An' we can both shoot the eye out've a sparrow at fifty yards whilst he's a-flyin'.'

The argument between the mayor of Prosper Gulch and his sons went on at length, but only consisted of restating the same positions over and over. Finally Art threw up his hands. 'Oh, all right! You can go. But I want you to take the dog, and I want you both to take your guns and plenty of ammunition. And start early, so you can make sure you get past Lodge Pole Ridge before dark.'

Josiah and Isaiah, at fourteen and thirteen, were as tall as their father, well muscled, and every bit as much at home in the mountains and the timber as they were in town.

The sun hadn't quite crept above the eastern horizon when the boys rode out of town. They rode mottled mustangs and led a packhorse with their camping gear. A delighted mongrel dog trotted alongside, thrilled that he got to accompany the boys on one of their outings. Most of the time they groused about his exuberance scaring away all the wildlife before they even had a chance to sneak up on it and watch it, and they refused to take him.

They had been able to watch some remarkable things. On one trip they had chanced upon a doe mule deer in a canyon bottom that seemed to be the appointed nursemaid for other does. She was watching over six spotted fawns. They crept close enough to watch them as the fawns played. Their most delightful game developed when one of them climbed a large boulder that bulged from the canyon side. From the top of the boulder he jumped as far out as he could, onto the canyon floor. Immediately another fawn climbed up and made the same jump, obviously trying to outdo the jump of the first one. The game was on at once. As if by careful organization, a line of fawns formed, climbing up to the flat spot on top of the boulder and jumping as far as they could. They continued the game for a quarter of an hour.

A sound that neither boy could hear from up the canyon brought the doe to attention. She instantly herded all the fawns into a thick patch of brush. The fawns understood the fear she somehow telegraphed to them. They lay down flat in the brush, and simply disappeared. Their spotted coats blended so perfectly that neither boy could see a one of them, even though they had watched them lie down and knew exactly where they were. The doe stood uncertainly in the middle of the canyon bottom for a full minute, then bounded off toward the south and west. The boys had stayed where they were, not moving, not making a sound.

Minutes later a slight movement on the opposite canyon rim caught their attention. A mountain lion glided between trees and rocks, working his way along, halfway down the far side of the canyon. Certain the big cat would spot the fawns and kill them all, Isaiah started to move his rifle forward. A quick, silent squeeze of his arm from Josiah stopped him. They watched breathlessly.

The cougar was halfway to the canyon floor when it caught the fresh scent of the doe. Its ears jerked forward. Its tail went motionless, nearly touching the ground, then curling up at the end. It studied the scent on the wind a long moment, then leaped to the canyon floor and swiftly began to follow the unseen trail of the doe.

'Wow!' Isaiah breathed when the cat was well out of sight. 'How's come he didn't smell them fawns?'

'The fawns don't have any scent for him to smell,' Josiah sagely informed him.

'They don't?'

'Nope.'

'How come?'

Josiah shrugged. 'God's way o' protectin' 'em, I 'spect. They're helpless. They can't run fast enough to get away from nothin'. They can't fight off nothin'. So till they lose their spots, they ain't got no scent. I watched a catamount walk past ten feet from a fawn that was hid, once, and he never did know it was there.'

'No kiddin'?'

'No kiddin'.'

'Did you shoot the mountain lion?'

'That's the hide Ma's got on the livin' room floor.'

As they launched forth on their newest adventure, both hoped for an experience that would be at least as memorable as that one. This trip, however, seemed ill-fated from the beginning. They were scarcely two miles out of Prosper Gulch when Josiah's horse began to limp. Josiah stopped, dismounted, and inspected the horse's foot. A small pebble had managed to lodge under the horseshoe on his right front hoof. With the point of his knife, Josiah removed the rock, and the horse seemed OK, though he continued to favor that leg slightly. It wasn't much, but it was just enough to slow them slightly.

Less than a mile later, their dog tangled with a porcupine as he explored a patch of brush. Yelping and howling, he returned to the boys. His face bristled with quills. Isaiah sat down on the ground, pulled the dog onto his lap, wrapped his arms around him, and held him while Josiah methodically pulled the quills.

'Don't bust any of 'em off, Joe,' Isaiah cautioned. 'They'll just keep on workin' deeper if you leave part of any of 'em in there.'

'You think I don't know that, Ike?' Josiah growled. 'I don't want him to end up like Rags did.'

'Yeah,' Isaiah agreed. 'It pertneart busted my heart watchin' that lump grow on his throat from the quill that busted off an' Pa couldn't get out. Then he got where he couldn't swallow, an' Pa had to shoot 'im, to put 'im out've his misery. We sure don't want that happenin' to Scruffy.'

It took the better part of an hour before they had all the quills out and could resume their trip. The dog, however, had lost his exuberance. He trotted along behind Joe's horse, his tail between his legs and his head down. Two hours later Isaiah landed in the cactus. He was just reaching down to pull out a large cockle burr that had lodged in the cuff of his pants, when a jackrabbit exploded out of a clump of sage brush. His mustang shied, jumping several feet to the left. Isaiah didn't have a chance to stay in the saddle. He landed flat, right in a patch of low cactus with broad, flat leaves bristling with two-inch needle-sharp stickers. He let out a howl, and rolled over to escape the cactus. As he did, he embedded even more stickers in the side of his hip and leg. It took another full hour to remove all the stickers from his body and his clothing.

Those who have never suffered such an injury don't understand the venom of cactus. The needles of a cactus not only stick and puncture. Each also contains minute amounts of secretion that make the wound they inflict sting and hurt, even after they are removed. Large numbers of them have as profound an effect on the victim's general health as numerous bee or hornet stings. It was clearly evident that Isaiah was not feeling well by the time the stickers were all removed.

'Maybe we'd best just go back home,' Josiah suggested.

'No way!' Isaiah protested. 'I ain't goin' back home with my tail betwixt my legs just cause I got dumped in a stupid cactus patch.'

'You don't look too pert, though.'

'I'm fine! Let's get movin'. We've lost too much time already.'

Josiah looked like he was going to argue, then shrugged his shoulders instead.

They made better time after that. It didn't matter. They had already lost too much time to get as far as they had planned. The sun was reaching for the western mountains when Josiah said,

'We ain't gonna make the high spring afore dark.'

'Nope. Not even close.'

'We'd best be findin' a spot to camp.'

'Yeah, but not just any spot. We ain't past where the killin's been happenin'.'

'That's what worries me. I hate to admit Pa was right, but I 'spect he was.'

'Do you remember that spot up high on Thistle Crick?'

'What spot?'

'The spot where that big ol' cliff makes a big bend.'

'Yeah. What about it?'

'Seems to me that'd make a perfect place to camp.'

'Why? The ground ain't nowhere's near level. Slopes plumb away toward the crick. And it's all covered with that scrubby brush. There ain't hardly a clear spot to even lie down.'

'Yeah, but the way that cliff curls around that one spot, there ain't no way anything could get at us from three sides. We'd only have to watch one side. There'll be a moon by midnight. If anything tries to sneak up on us, it'll make all kinds o' noise gettin' through all that brush.'

'Unless what's been doin' all them killin's ain't normal.'

'You mean somethin' unnatural?'

'That's exactly what I mean. If's it's straight outa hell, it won't hafta sneak up on us. It'll just pop up right in front of us, afore we even know it's comin'.'

'Do you really think it is?'

A long, uncomfortable silence settled around them for nearly a mile. Finally, Josiah said, 'No, I guess I don't. Not really. I sure don't know what it is, but I don't guess I believe in devils bein' able to get outa hell an' kill folks. If they could, there'd be hundreds o' dead folks showin' up all the time.'

'Then let's camp at that spot.'

'What are we goin' to do with the horses?'

'Make 'em stay with us.'

'And eat brush all night?'

'Better'n gettin' their throats tore out.'

After another long silence, Josiah

said, 'Well, let's look that spot over.'

It was less than an hour before dark when they reached the place. It was exactly as Isaiah had remembered. It was a poor and uncomfortable place to camp, but it offered as good a protection as they could ask. There was even a small patch of open grass close to the cliff where they could picket the horses. At least they could crop enough grass to keep them going for another day.

They spread their bed rolls right against the cliff. They fixed themselves some supper and coffee over a small fire, then put it out carefully. By that time it was fully dark. Each boy checked his rifle. Josiah sat down on his blankets and leaned back against the wall of the cliff. Scruffy lay down against him, with his nose resting on Josiah's leg. 'You ain't goin' to bed?' Isaiah asked.

'Not yet,' Josiah replied. 'Ain't sleepy just yet. I 'spect I'll sit here an' watch an' listen awhile.'

'Me too,' Isaiah agreed. 'I ain't scared, mind you, but I ain't sleepy just yet.'

Both boys sat perfectly still, listening intently as the darkness deepened. Neither boy knew when he drifted off to sleep. It was still a couple hours short of midnight when a sudden shift of breeze brought Scruffy fully alert. He stiffened. His head came up. A low growl, barely audible, rumbled in his throat. At the same time two of the horses snorted. Both boys jerked awake instantly. As if controlled by one volition, both boys jerked their rifles to their shoulders. Scruffy shot forward, disappearing into the night.

Almost instantly Josiah whistled sharply. Brush crashed two dozen yards away from them in the darkness, its noise exaggerated by the otherwise stillness of the night. Both boys began firing their rifles wildly into the darkness in the general direction of the noise. When they ran out of ammunition, Josiah went about reloading as swiftly as his trembling hands allowed. Isaiah simply continued to squeeze his rifle's trigger, work the lever, squeeze the trigger, oblivious to the fact that his gun's firing pin was falling on an empty chamber.

'Ike! Reload!' Josiah commanded, his voice soft but edged with authority.

The voice broke through Isaiah's panic. He stopped trying to fire the empty weapon and began to reload. Crackling in the brush nearly brought a renewed volley of fire from the boys before Josiah whispered, 'Don't shoot. It's Scruffy.'

The dog crawled back to Josiah, bleeding badly. Josiah dropped his gun and began feeling around on the dog, trying to learn the extent of his injuries. He appeared to have only one long gash, starting at the base of his throat and running across his shoulder. Josiah whipped his shirt off and used it to bind up the dog's wound as best as he could. The horses were snorting and squealing, fighting against the picket ropes that tethered them near the cliff.

'Let's move over by the horses,' Josiah whispered.

Carrying his rifle and the dog, he

moved that direction. Isaiah followed, crabbing sideways, peering intently into the darkness, straining to hear, fighting hard against the panic that threatened to rob him of reason. Laying the dog against the base of the cliff, Josiah moved among the horses, petting and calming them. They responded to his touch, settling down almost at once. Isaiah was slower to return to normal. His voice quivered when he eventually spoke in a hoarse whisper. 'You think it's gone?'

'Yup.'

'How can you tell?'

'Scruffy ain't got his hackles up no more. The horses wouldn'ta let me calm 'em down that quick if they could still smell whatever it was.'

'Whatd'ya think it was?'

Josiah didn't answer. He didn't have an answer. Two hours later, when the full moon lifted above the horizon, it seemed like the welcome advent of daylight to two frightened boys whose eyes ached from straining into the darkness.

'I don't see nothin',' Isaiah offered finally.

'Whatever it was, it's gone,' Josiah agreed.

'You 'spect it'll come back?'

'Don't know.'

'I think we oughta get outa here.'

'Me too. Keep your eyes peeled. I'll saddle the horses and load our stuff.'

Half an hour later they rode out of the shelter of the protecting cliffs. Josiah held the wounded dog across his legs, and watched his horse's ears carefully. He was certain the horse would detect a return of whatever had tried to attack them before he would. With hearts hammering, they rode back and forth in the general area from which the sounds of the night had emanated. They found nothing.

'Whatever it was, we sure didn't kill it.'

'Nope. Must've scared it off, though.'

'We've spent enough time lookin'. I'm gettin' outa here.'

'Keep your eyes peeled.'

The sun was just chasing the last of the night's shadows from the land when they rode back into Prosper Gulch. They did their best to ride tall and brave until they came into sight of their house. Then they lost all pretense and kicked the horses into a run, skidding to a stop in a cloud of dust by their front porch. It would be a very long time before either boy suggested a camping trip in the mountains. It would be far less time before they began to realize how incredibly fortunate they had been.

8

'You oughta know what it is, Whoosh-tay.'

The old Lakota looked across the saloon at the man who had called out to him. He visibly weighed whether he was being asked for an opinion, or was about to be the subject of a typical cowboy's jest. Whatever he saw in the speaker's face seemed to invite him to offer an opinion. Clearly hopeful that doing so might result in a free drink, he walked toward the three men at the table. He walked with a rolling gate, his legs so badly bowed a dog could have run between his knees while his feet were held tightly together. He had been a fearsome warrior in his day, but time had taken a heavy toll on his body. His gait as he crossed the saloon validated his name. 'Whooshtay', in the Lakota tongue, meant 'Bad Legs'.

Those who didn't use the Lakota name usually just called him 'Legs'.

He sat down at the table in the chair one of the men scooted out with a foot in invitation. 'Do you know what it is?' the man who had originally spoken asked.

Whooshtay failed to answer. Instead, he looked meaningfully at the mugs of beer each of the men held cradled in work roughened hands. The speaker caught on at once. He turned toward the bar and called out, 'Hey, Toby! Bring Legs a beer, would ya?'

'Not a chance.'

'What?'

'I can't sell liquor to no Indian. You know that.'

'Well, bring me another beer, then.'

The bartender only hesitated a moment. 'I s'pose you want a clean mug, too?'

'Yeah, now that you mention it. This here one's got slobbers all over it.'

A couple minutes later the bartender sat the beer on the table and picked up the man's nickel. 'Just don't let me see you givin' that Indian any of it, Flint,' he admonished piously. 'If I see you do that, I'll have to report you to the marshal.'

'I wouldn't dream o' doin' nothin' against the law,' Flint replied with a straight face.

When Toby retreated to behind the bar, Flint slid the mug of beer over in front of Whooshtay. He grabbed it and drank half of it in one breath. He set the mug down and leaned back, wiping his mouth with the back of his hand. 'Well,' Flint demanded. 'Whatd'ya know about what's doin' all these killin's?'

Whooshtay looked around the table, fixing each man in turn with a gaze that had suddenly regained some of the steely fire that had struck fear into hearts in his younger days. When he spoke, it was slowly, his voice heavily accented, the consonants accented just a little too much. 'It is a story I have heard many times in the lodges of my people. It is told again in the nights when strange howls carry on the winds, and when things happen that men cannot explain.

'Many winters ago, before any white men came except the buffalo hunters, there was a young girl in the village of Wild Heart. She was very beautiful. Her father, Wild Heart, was chief of the village. He loved her very much. Her name was Wind Flower.

'When Wind Flower was just able to begin to walk, Wild Heart found a white puppy. He found it in a place where there had been some kind of a fight. There was much blood on the ground, but nothing was left of whatever had fought. The grass and the brush had been trampled and broken for a long way around. When Wild Heart was walking away, he saw a little movement in the brush, and turned aside to see what it was. Then it was that he found the puppy. He did not know whether it was a dog puppy, or a wolf puppy, or what it was, but it was pure white. A pure white animal is good medicine. Very strong medicine. It seemed to him to be a gift of the gods. So Wild Heart picked it up and took it home with him.

'He brought it into his tepee, even though the Lakota never let their dogs into their tepees. When he brought it in and set it on the ground, Wind Flower said her first word. She said, 'Sunka Wanagi — Ghost Dog.'

'The puppy went straight to her and licked her hand. So it became her dog. Because it was pure white, like a ghost, Wild Heart declared that Wind Flower had named it right. It's name became Sunka Wanagi.

'The dog grew very big. Very strong. Its head was very large and its eyes were bright. It went with Wind Flower everywhere she went. If she told it to do so, it would chase down a deer, or even a full-grown elk. Some said it would even kill a small tatanka — a small buffalo — but I never believed that.

'By the time Wind Flower had grown into a beautiful young woman, the dog should have been old enough to die. But he was just as swift and strong as when he was young. There was no place Wild Heart was afraid to send his daughter, because Sunka Wanagi was always with her, and nothing could harm her.

'But one day when she had gone a long way away from the village, some buffalo hunters saw the two of them. There were five of them. One of them shot Sunka Wanagi, from farther away than Wind Flower knew a gun would reach. The bullet did not kill Sunka Wanagi, but it crippled him.

'Wind Flower was frantic, because the dog was more important to her than anything in the world. She started trying to stop its bleeding, to take care of it. But the buffalo hunters grabbed her. When they saw how much she loved the dog, they decided to make a sport of her love for her dog. They tied her up and made her watch, while they tortured the dog until he died. Then they took turns raping her, until they could do so no more. They tortured her to death as well.

'When Wind Flower did not come home, Wild Heart went to find her. He found her and Sunka Wanagi. He read the sign, and knew what had happened. He set out to track the buffalo hunters, to avenge what they had done.

'They knew they would be pursued, so they ran a long way away, as fast as they could go. It was four moons before Wild Heart finally caught up to them. Because they knew he was following them, they traveled in a big circle to confuse him. Eventually they came back to the place where they had done all those things.

'It was there that Wild Heart finally found them. But he did not kill them. They were all dead when he found them. All five of them had had their throats ripped out by something that had caught them too quickly for them even to fire a gun or draw a knife to defend themselves.

'Wild Heart took their scalps and

buried them with Wind Flower and Sunka Wanagi, whom he had buried together. Then he asked the medicine man to make a special curse that would bring Sunka Wanagi back if any white people ever tried to live in the place where the buffalo hunters had done all those terrible things.

'I did not know where that place was until I began to hear the stories of what has been happening in that area. But when first I began to hear the stories, I knew right away what it was. It is Sunka Wanagi. It is Ghost Dog. It is his spirit, which takes vengeance on any white person that trespasses onto the land that he guards, or on any white people who try to settle too close to that area. That is why nobody has ever seen what attacks. It is Sunka Wanagi. It is Ghost Dog.'

Nobody had ever heard Whooshtay say more than half a dozen words at one time. The three men sat, spellbound, as he related the story. By the time he had finished a dozen others had gathered around, hanging on every word. When he finished, Whooshtay stood and bowlegged his way across the saloon and out the back door. Deathly silence settled on the entire saloon.

After several minutes, Flint said, 'He didn't even finish his beer.'

All eyes swivelled to the half-full beer mug that sat untouched. 'I never knew Legs to leave a drop of any kind of booze in anything,' somebody said.

Nobody laughed. Nobody offered any derisive comments about superstition. Nobody offered any further comment. It seemed as if a great white ghost dog suddenly haunted every mind.

9

'How long do you intend to stay, Mr — ' The desk clerk looked down at the registry, 'Mr Hoover?'

Art Hoover's sigh revealed both his weariness and his low spirits. 'I'm not sure. That will depend on a number of things. I am seeking a man by the name of Pat Harmon. I was told he might also be staying here.'

The clerk nodded. 'Yup. Pat's been holed up here for a while. Gettin' itchy feet, though, if I know Pat.'

Art brightened perceptibly. 'You know him?'

'Sure thing. Everybody in these parts does. I've known him since he rode into town. Came here to clean up our town, you know.'

'I had heard that, as a matter of fact. And I presume he did so?'

'You better believe it. He's really

somethin', Pat is. This here town had been held by the short hairs for a long spell, and nobody knew who was behind it. It didn't take Pat more'n a month to get to the bottom of it. When he got it figured out, he cleaned out the whole rat's nest, almost single handed.'

'His investigation resulted in a fight, I take it?'

'More like a small war, if you really want to know. Bryce Schilling had a small army workin' for 'im, he did. Didn't do him no good, though, once Pat got stuff figured out.'

'So you're telling me this one man engaged with a well-entrenched criminal who had a small army at his disposal, and emerged victorious?'

The clerk grinned with obvious relish. 'That's what happened. Oh, he had some of the town folks whom he knew he could trust involved, but it was him that did almost all of it. Hell on high red wheels, that man is. He hunted down Red Atkins and killed him in a stand-up shootout just afore he took the job o' cleanin' up our town. I'd sooner face the devil himself than Pat Harmon.'

Art pursed his lips thoughtfully. 'That seems to be pretty much the story we heard as well. I assumed it was greatly exaggerated, but at least worthy of some credibility.'

'Better'n that, Mr — Hoover. Better'n that. It's gospel, what I'm tellin' you. I seen part of it with my own eyes.'

'I see. And could you tell me where I might find Mr Harmon?'

The clerk frowned thoughtfully. 'Not off hand. He's been ridin' off somewhere about every day. He's usually back by this time, though. Did you walk up here from the livery barn, by any chance?'

'Well, yes. I left my horse and buggy there.'

'Did you happen to see a big dapple-gray gelding tied up along the street? There would likely have been a big ugly dog with him.'

'Hmm. Yes, as a matter of fact, I did. Right in front of the café down the street, as I remember. Very large dog.

96

Shaggy fellow. A mongrel of some sort, it appeared.'

'Yup. That'd be him. That'd mean Pat's in the café grabbin' a bite to eat. That dog goes everywhere with him, except inside. The only place he goes inside is here. The dog stays in the room with him. Everywhere else, the dog just lies outside the door, waitin' for Pat to come back out.'

'I see. Well, I shall take my valise up to my room, then I'll see if I can find Mr Harmon.'

Fifteen minutes later Art Hoover approached the business boasting a sign with the single word, 'Café'. As he neared the place a very large man riding a chestnut mare approached the hitching rail in front of the place. His long hair and full beard emphasized both his size and his lack of grooming. His clothes were dirty. His half buttoned shirt hung outside his pants. The long underwear beneath it only got washed if its wearer accidentally fell into the water. He stepped from the saddle with a lithe grace that his appearance belied. His path to the door of the café was blocked by the large shaggy dog, lying placidly beside the gelding.

Without a word the man swung a booted foot to kick the dog out of his way. The dog was not nearly as inattentive as he had appeared. From lying flat in the dirt he leaped sideways, under the gelding, deftly avoiding the foot that would have lifted him clear across the sidewalk. The force of the kick nearly caused the man to fall. He took a quick step backward and grabbed the cantle of his saddle to keep his balance. A passing cowboy laughed aloud. 'Quicker'n he looks, ain't he?'

The big man stopped abruptly. His face reddened. He glanced at the mocking cowboy, then glared at the dog, which was now lying down on the other side of the gelding, watching him with apparent unconcern. 'You worthless cur,' he gritted, 'no stray mongrel's gonna get away with makin' Mike Mulligan look like a fool.'

He grabbed for his gun. The dog instantly moved to a crouch, as if ready to spring. It was the voice that stopped his draw, however. From the sidewalk a soft voice with an unmistakably hard edge said, 'I wouldn't do that, if I were you. If you pull your gun after tryin' to kick that dog, he'll take it away from you and tear your arm half off doin' it. He's a whole lot faster'n he looks.'

His gun half-out of the holster, Mulligan turned his attention to the speaker. The man on the sidewalk was as tall as his own six foot three. His shoulders were at least as broad. That was where the similarity ended. He was lean hipped, and his stomach betrayed none of the soft bulge that Mulligan sported. He was dressed neatly in clean clothes, well shaven, holding a tooth-pick in the corner of his mouth. 'Who're you?' Mulligan demanded. 'Do you own that mongrel?'

The man smiled easily. 'Well, now, I'm not just real sure. I never have been sure whether I own him or he owns me.

We sorta belong together, though.'

'Stupid mutt made a fool outa me,' Mulligan declared.

The man laughed softly. 'Well, now, he can do a lot of things, but I don't think that's one of them. Nobody has the ability to make a fool out of someone else. He does have a way of showin' up someone who already is a fool, though.'

Mulligan's face reddened even more. 'Are you callin' me a fool?'

'You brought it up,' the man replied. 'I sure wouldn't argue with the assessment, though.'

That offered Mulligan exactly the focus for his embarrassment and anger he needed. With a low growl that sounded more animal than human, he took three swift steps up onto the sidewalk and sent a surprisingly fast right fist at the face of the newcomer who had dared to taunt him. Quick as the blow was, the man easily stepped inside it, brushing it away with his left hand at the same time that his own right hand delivered a sledge-hammer blow to the soft midsection of the big Irishman. A second, then a third blow followed it to the same target before Mulligan could react or slow his forward momentum.

He recovered quickly, however, and sent a hard, chopping left hook at the side of the head of his surprising adversary. Like his first attempt, it wasn't nearly quick enough. The second man had already stepped back and to one side, letting the huge fist pass in front of his nose. He came back in right behind it, sending two swift blows, one with each fist, to the brows of the man's eyes. Blood gushed behind the fists, and began to flow copiously downward.

It was nothing but a mild, almost surgical exercise for the other man after that. Unable to keep his eyes clear of blood, Mulligan thrashed blindly at where the other man should have been. All the while, that other man, with methodical and pinpoint accuracy, reduced Mulligan's face to mincemeat. When he tired of it, the man said, in a calm, conversational voice, 'Aw, that's enough, I guess.'

As he said it, he ducked under a big roundhouse right that vainly sought to connect with something. From the ground, the man brought up a straight overhand right that connected with Mulligan's chin, making a sound like a watermelon smashing on a flat rock. Mulligan's head rocked back from the blow. Then the rest of his body followed. He landed on the sidewalk, sprawled spread-eagled, unconscious. The other man didn't seem to notice. By the time Mulligan hit the sidewalk, he had already turned away, his attention swinging to the dog. He stepped off the sidewalk and held out a hand. The dog rose and came to him. He stopped right in front of him, sat down, and looked up expectantly.

'You did good, Dougly,' the man said. 'Maybe I shoulda just stayed out of it and let you take care of him. I did need the exercise, though.'

He petted the dog briefly, then

straightened and prepared to mount the gelding.

'Excuse me. Are you Patrick Harmon?'

The man stopped, one foot already in the stirrup, and eyed the speaker. 'Only when my ma was mad at me,' he replied. 'The rest of the time I'm just Pat.'

Art Hoover grinned. 'I can relate to that,' he said. 'The only two people that ever called me 'Arthur' were my ma and the preacher. I never was sure which one I was most afraid of when they did.'

'What can I do for you?' Harmon replied, removing his foot from the stirrup.

'I wonder if I might speak with you. My name is Art Hoover. I am the mayor of a town named Prosper Gulch, a little over a hundred miles from here.'

Harmon studied him carefully for a long moment, then said, 'I've heard of it. Are you buyin' the coffee?'

'Of course.'

'Well, in that case, I guess we could talk.'

When they were in the café, at a

corner table away from the door, each holding a cup of steaming coffee with both hands, Art said, 'I understand you have considerable prowess as both a detective and a fighting man. I can attest to the latter, by the way. That was an absolutely masterful job of dealing with the gentleman who tried to kick your dog.'

'I don't know that I'd call him a gentleman. He was too mad to fight well,' Pat replied. 'He was a whole lot quicker than he looked like he'd be, though.'

'So is that dog. Did I hear you call him 'Dougly'?'

'Yup.'

'That's a rather strange name. I don't believe I've heard it before.'

'Well, I started out callin' him 'Dumb And Ugly', but that takes a lot o' wind, just callin' 'im. So I sorta shortened it to 'Dougly'.'

Hoover chuckled with appreciation of the humor. 'Well, I don't suppose he probably minds either one.'

'He hasn't given up ownin' me, anyway.'

Art abruptly addressed the purpose of his presence there. 'Would you, by any chance, be interested in a job?'

Pat studied him over the rim of his coffee cup as he sipped the scalding liquid. He put the cup back on the table. 'Talk to me.'

Taken aback for the barest instant by the unexpected response, Art launched into his well-rehearsed speech. He had been running it over and over in his mind all the way from Prosper Gulch. 'Well, as I said, I'm the mayor of Prosper Gulch. For the past few months we have had a very dire and mysterious problem. People are getting killed, and we have absolutely no idea who or what is doing it.'

Pat took another sip of coffee as he studied the mayor, but offered no comment, so Art continued. 'It started with a homesteader. Single fellow. Nice guy. Someone found him behind his house — well, more of a shack, actually, as so many homesteads are — with his throat torn out.'

'Torn out?'

'Yes. There was practically nothing left between his chin and his chest, as if some very large animal had grabbed him by the throat and just ripped it away.'

'Was he eaten on some?'

'That's one of the mysteries. He was untouched, except for that one wound.'

'That's strange.'

'Strange, yes. Frightening as well. And rather signature, I'm afraid.'

'Signature?'

'It has become a pattern. A young cowboy and his dog, camping alone in the area near that homestead, were killed in the same manner.'

'Him and his dog both?'

'Both of them. Then a pair of young people from a wagon train were killed in exactly the same manner. Both at exactly the same time. They sneaked away from the wagons in the night, apparently for a tryst. One of the guards heard a small noise he couldn't identify. Thinking it might be Indians trying to sneak up on them in the darkness, he alerted others. A party of men found the couple. Both of them were killed in that same signature way.'

'But neither one of 'em had yelled or anything?'

'There was virtually no sound, except that one small noise the guard heard.'

'Has anybody this thing attacked survived an attack?'

'Well, yes. At least we think so. There is an old cowboy on the LRH ranch who was, we presumed, targeted by whatever it is. He believes his pet tomcat surprised it, attacked it, and it apparently fled.'

Pat's eyebrows rose in a high arch. 'A cat?'

Hoover smiled wryly. 'He adopted a very large tomcat that strayed into the ranch. It's a frightfully ugly and ill-tempered beast, universally hated by every hand on the ranch except old Clyde. But it accompanies Clyde everywhere, either running alongside him, or riding on top of his bedroll.'

Harmon laughed aloud. 'That must be somethin' to see. A tough old broken down cowpoke with a cat ridin' shotgun.'

Art smiled in spite of the somber nature of the things he had been relating. 'They do make an interesting pair.'

'Has anyone else been close to whatever this is and lived to tell about it?'

Art sat up a bit straighter and cleared his throat. 'There are my two sons.'

'Your sons?'

Hoover nodded. 'I have two sons. Josiah is fourteen, going on fifteen. Isaiah is thirteen. They fancy themselves something of mountain men, as boys that age often do. They were intending to pass through the area where these things have been happening, while it was still during daylight hours — '

'This thing only attacks at night?'

'Yes. Always. Well, so far as we know, anyway. At night, when there is no moon, as nearly as we have been able to ascertain.'

'So the boys didn't get past the area before dark?'

'No. Due to a number of things — their dog got into a porcupine, and some things — so they camped at a place where they felt they were well defended and nothing could sneak up on them in the dark.'

'But it did?'

'It tried. At least they are both convinced it did. Their dog alerted them, and they thought they heard something. Their horses caught scent of something as well, and started fighting against their pickets. They panicked, and started shooting blindly into the darkness. They think their shooting frightened it away.'

'But they didn't hit it?'

'No. They looked, but found no sign of anything. Whatever it was made one big gash on the dog. It started at the base of his throat and ran clear across his shoulder, as if a large tooth or claw came very close to missing him. Or very close to killing him.'

Pat sipped on his coffee, frowning in concentration. Art did not interrupt his thoughts. At last Pat said, 'Has there been any bunch of unsolved crimes anywhere in the area?'

Art frowned. 'Not that I've heard of. What would that have to do with whatever we're facing, though?'

'Just thinkin'. If a bunch of outlaws found a good hideout and didn't want anyone stumblin' onto it, they might dream up somethin' like that to keep folks scared away.'

'Ah! I hadn't thought of that possibility at all. It had not occurred to me that it might be a person or people. It happens so silently, and it has all the marks of a large animal. Or something not human, at least.'

'What would be not human but not animal either?'

Art cleared his throat again. Looking almost embarrassed, he said, 'Well, there is quite a lot of talk around town of an ancient curse.'

'Curse?'

Hoover took a deep breath. 'There is an old Indian who lives in town. He tells a story of a young Indian girl who was raped and murdered by buffalo hunters. She had a very large dog that went everywhere with her as her guard. They took great delight in forcing her to watch them torture and kill the dog before they turned their attentions to her. The Indian legend that Legs — his real name is Whooshtay. That means 'bad legs'. He's quite crippled. The legend that he has been telling is that her dog became a ghost dog that kills any white people who linger in the area where the killings happened. There are a lot of people who believe the legend has merit. They think it is Sunka Wanagi. Ghost Dog.'

'How about you?'

Silence held the floor with eloquence for a long moment. Then Art said, 'I am a Christian. I have little inclination to believe in ghosts, human or animal.'

'How about demons?'

Art's eyebrows rose abruptly. After

another long silence, he said, 'Nor demons, I think. My boys' wild shooting into the darkness would hardly have banished demons.'

'How many folks have been killed?'

'More than a dozen, that we know of. There may have been others passing through that we don't know about, whose bodies have not yet been discovered.'

Pat's response came more as a statement than a question. 'So you want me to ride up there and chase down whatever man or animal or demon is killin' folks, even though nobody's seen it and nobody knows what it is, and just single-handedly put a stop to the whole business.'

Art nodded as if oblivious to the sarcasm in Pat's response. 'Several of the businessmen and a number of ranchers have grouped together to hire someone who's capable of doing so. We will pay one hundred dollars a month, plus a bonus of five hundred dollars for clear evidence of who or what is doing the killing, plus an additional five hundred dollars if that person or thing is . . . eliminated.'

Pat whistled. 'That's a lot of money.'

Art nodded. 'We are asking a lot.'

As if he had long since made his decision, Pat said, 'I thought it was about time I was movin' on from here.'

10

The westering sun forced him to pull his hat brim down farther than normal. With his eyes shaded by it, Pat Harmon surveyed the ranch yard that lay uphill, a quarter mile from where he sat his horse. It had been a long ride. He was tired, dusty, hungry and dry. Even so, he had no intention of riding into a strange ranch without carefully studying its layout. Everything he saw sparked approval in his mind. The whole ranch yard was positioned east of a series of tall peaks that would shelter it from the worst of winter winds. Though north winds were always cold, the worst of their storms inevitably blew in from the southwest.

While sheltered from those winds, the ranch was built far enough from those towering peaks to be well out of danger of the snow avalanches the high country was prone to in heavy winters. Cascading down the steep slopes like a hundred freight trains, those avalanches were capable of sweeping away forests and burying anything in their path. More than a few mining towns had been wiped off the map by that very phenomenon. Even so, in greedy defiance of the dangers, mining towns continued to spring up in every canyon where gold or silver was found.

The LRH ranch yard he surveyed had clearly taken that risk into account, and had been built accordingly. At the same time, it was backed by treeless slopes and talus that made it defensible from all directions. Although in tall timber country, the area for 300 yards around the yard was treed sparsely enough to prevent the furtive approach of attackers, or threat from forest fire. Trees that were allowed to grow provided welcome shade without the dangers inherent in thick forests.

The buildings reflected the same careful planning. The ranch house itself was large, solidly built of native stones and logs. Tall, narrow windows boasted heavy shutters that could be closed in the event of an Indian attack, which all hoped had become a thing of the past. Even so, the cross-shaped slots in each shutter bore witness to the ability of rifles to cover the entire field of fire from relative safety.

Across the ranch yard a long bunkhouse boasted three separate doors and the same tall windows with shutters fastened securely back against the walls. Between the bunkhouse and the corrals, a building that had to be the cook house squatted in the center of the yard. Smoke and the steady ringing of a hammer against an anvil indicated there was a blacksmith shop on the back side of the same building.

The horse barn was as large as any Pat had seen. His conservative guess of twenty stalls was short by half. In addition, the interior boasted a large granary for oats, an open space where cattle or horses could be worked on inside, out of inclement weather, and a hay mow capable of holding tons of hay. Pat's reflection was interrupted by a low, warning growl from Dougly. Glancing at the dog, Pat looked the way the dog was alerting. A lone rider approached through the timber.

'It's OK, Dougly,' Pat soothed. 'Don't look like trouble.' As the rider drew closer, he altered his estimation entirely. 'In fact, that looks like somethin' downright nice, or trouble of a whole different kind,' he said.

The rider approaching was a strikingly beautiful young woman. Curls of light, reddish-brown hair cascaded from beneath a worn Stetson, framing a face that had to come directly from every lonely cowboy's fondest dreams. A bridge of light freckles arched across her nose, as if drawing attention to the brilliant green of her eyes. Her near-perfect figure was enhanced, rather than disguised, by the man's corduroy trousers that were almost too tight, and the wool shirt whose buttons were challenged to remain closed.

Pat swept his own hat off as she approached. She responded with a broad, easy grin. 'Admiring the layout?' she asked, as she reined her horse in beside him.

'I was till you rode up and gave me something better to admire,' Pat replied.

Trying her best to ignore the redness that instantly brightened her cheeks, she said, 'It's just about the most perfect setting a ranch could have, isn't it?'

Pat considered another pointed remark, but decided not to press his luck. He reluctantly turned his eyes back to the ranch yard. 'I haven't been able to think of one thing anyone could do that would improve it,' he acknowledged. 'Whoever built it, sure knew what he was doing.'

'My father,' she said, without affectation.

Pat extended a hand. 'My name's Pat Harmon.'

She reached out and took the hand in as firm a grip as a man's handshake would be expected to have. 'Callie Hebert,' she replied, pronouncing the name as if it were spelled 'Hibbert,' rather than 'Hey bear,' as Pat would have guessed. He was totally unprepared for the feeling that swept over him. As their hands met and gripped each other's, he looked into her eyes. He would never be able to describe the sensation of that moment. Her eyes widened slightly, as they do when one unexpectedly spies an old and dear friend. Her mouth opened slightly. His throat tightened. He felt, for a moment, as if he couldn't breathe. They continued to stare into each other's eyes for half a minute, unaware of the passing of time.

Then the moment was gone. He released her hand. She withdrew her own, looking self-conscious, almost frightened. 'Callie,' he pondered. 'That short for something?'

She reddened again, ever so slightly, as she nodded. She cleared her throat, as if she were having a small difficulty speaking. 'Uh, yeah. Yeah, it's short for 'Calico', but I don't care much for being confused with a piece of cloth. Are you, uh, here looking for a job?'

He shook his head. 'Not really. I guess I got one, but it's probably more job than I can handle.'

Recognition flashed in Callie's eyes. 'Pat Harmon! That's why your name sounded familiar. You're the one that Art Hoover went to find.'

Pat nodded. 'He found me, I'm afraid.'

'And you've taken the job? Well, that's a dumb question. You're here.'

'I've taken the job. What do you know about the stuff goin' on?'

'The killings? Nothing you haven't already heard, I'm afraid. I don't even know where you'd start, trying to solve something like this. It has everybody scared to death.'

'Except you,' he replied very pointedly.

'What do you mean?'

'I mean it appears to me that you've been out riding in the timber by yourself. That doesn't indicate a whole lot of fear.'

'It's daylight. You won't likely find me

out alone after dark, even this close to the house. Even if Father would allow it. Which he wouldn't. But I love to ride, and I can check on the cattle as well as any of the other hands, so I'm not going to stop being out in the daytime.'

'What do you think's behind it?' he tossed at her abruptly.

The question caught her off guard. 'Folks don't usually ask my opinion.'

'I just did.'

'Well, then you'll get it. I think somebody wants the country to himself, so he's killing enough people to cause enough panic to get everyone else to leave.'

'Who would be doing that?'

'That's what you've been hired to find out,' she shot back.

He grinned. 'Nuts. I thought I might've just stumbled onto the one person that'd tell me the answer to the whole thing.'

Her smile in response lit up more than her face. Something in that smile lit the deep and lonely parts of his innermost being. Her eyes danced as she responded. 'You're lucky I don't know that much. Just think what that'd do to your reputation if some weak and ignorant woman solved the whole thing before you could even get started.'

'Somehow, I doubt that you're either of them two things, but if you had the whole thing figured out, that'd be just fine with me. I'm not exactly relishing the whole situation.'

'Then why did you take the job?'

Something in her tone telegraphed that she really wanted an honest answer to that, rather than another clever bit of repartee. He looked off across the ranch yard again for a long moment before answering. Then he said, 'In the first place, I just plain needed a job. Besides, it sounded like something that sure needed taking care of. If there was a chance I could stop folks from being killed but I just said 'No, thanks' when I was asked to help, I'd have a hard time shavin'.'

She frowned, her face darkening with confusion. 'Shaving?'

He grinned again. 'Gotta look in a mirror to shave decent. I like bein' able to look myself in the face without cringing.'

She smiled again as the reference clarified in her mind. 'Well, then, you'd just as well ride on in and I'll introduce you to my folks. Mother will have supper ready pretty soon.'

11

The low growl was the first indication of trouble. Pat turned in the saddle, his hand falling automatically to the butt of his gun. Dougly stood stock still. His tail was down, his head extended forward. The hair along his back stood straight up. He was staring fixedly at the ugliest apparition Pat could remember seeing.

It was a cat, or at least it had once resembled one. It was twice the size of a normal tomcat, easily the size of a bobcat. It was heavily scarred over much of its body. It stood facing Dougly. Its back was arched, the fur along its spine standing as rigidly as Dougly's hackles. The growl issuing from its throat was at least a match for that coming from the dog it faced.

Unexpectedly, the growls ceased. Each animal stared unmovingly at the other. Dougly took one stiff-legged step toward the cat, lowering his nose perceptibly. The move appeared more inquisitive than threatening. Callie acted as if she were about to intervene, but Pat held up a hand. 'Let 'em work it out,' he suggested.

She looked at him as if he had lost his mind. Twice she opened her mouth to explain the lunacy of such a suggestion, but each time she shut it again silently. Together they watched the tableau play out in front of them. The cat studied Dougly carefully for a full minute, then cocked his head slightly to one side. When he did, the dog took another tentative step toward him. As if somebody had flipped a hidden switch inside the cat's brain, its demeanor totally changed. The crooked tail began to sway slowly and rhythmically back and forth. The stiff arch left its back. Its hackles lay down as smoothly as anything on the decrepit looking creature could lie. It walked directly to the dog and lifted its nose to him.

Dougly reached out and touched noses with the strange looking beast. His own demeanor lost its truculence. He turned his back to the cat, sauntered over beside Pat's horse, and lay down. He looked up at Pat, his tongue hanging out of an open mouth that appeared for all the world to be grinning, panting happily. It was as if he were saying, 'Did you see that?'

In a surprise piled on top of surprise, the cat walked over and lay down almost against him, and began grooming himself contentedly. 'Well I'll be dad-gummed,' muttered a grizzled old cowboy, whom neither Pat nor Callie had seen approach.

Callie grinned broadly. 'Hey, Clyde. It looks like Sweetie Pie found a friend. Are you jealous?'

'Don't get smart with me, missy,' the old cowboy growled in feigned anger, jabbing a bony finger at her. 'I'm still able to turn you over my knee if I need to.'

She giggled in response. 'Seriously,

did you ever see him make up to a dog like that before?'

'I ain't never seen him make up to nothin' like that, 'cept me,' he admitted. He turned his attention to Pat. 'That your dog?'

'Either that or I'm his meal ticket,' Pat responded.

'What's his name?'

'Dougly.'

'Odd name.'

'Short for Dumb And Ugly.'

'Well, I guess you'll be renamin' 'im now.'

'Why's that?'

'Gonna be kinda hard to call anythin' ugly that's standin' beside Sweetie Pie.'

With a perfectly straight face, Pat said, 'Well, if that cat's Sweetie Pie, then my dog'll just figure that words mean the opposite and I'm really callin' him smart and beautiful.'

'Nope, that wouldn't never do,' Clyde rejected instantly. 'Only one around here fit to wear that handle is Callie, there.'

Pat's eyes shifted of their own volition to Callie's face. He said, 'I'll sure have to agree with that.'

He was rewarded with the first indication of a loss of words on her part. Her face reddened, but she seemed unable to retort. Her eyes that once again met his own answered more eloquently than words could have done in any case. Pat turned his attention back to the cowboy. 'Are you the one who had the run-in with the ghost dog, or whatever it is?'

'Sweetie Pie did, I reckon,' the cowboy drawled. 'I didn't see nothin' but a whole lot o' darkness, but he sure enough tangled with somethin'.'

'And lived to tell about it.'

'Well he lived, but he ain't told about it. Leastways, he ain't told me nothin'. He don't communicate too good, but he is some hard to kill.'

'He looks like the effort's been made a few times.'

'He does for a fact. I always figured that's why he picked me to ride with.

I'm the only one on the place as scarred up and ugly as he is.'

'Just as ugly, anyway,' Callie taunted him.

He glared at her in mock anger again, stabbing the air with that bony finger again. 'I'm tellin' you, missy, one more smart-aleck remark like that and I'll drag you off'n that horse and tan your hide.'

Pat interrupted the good-natured and obvious affectionate exchange. 'You didn't see or hear anything that'd indicate what it was, though, huh?'

Clyde turned his attention back to Pat. 'Nope. Why? Who are you and what is it to you?'

Callie answered for him. 'Clyde, this is Pat Harmon. He's the one folks sent for to try to find out who or what it is.'

Clyde's eyebrows rose. 'Oh, you're the hired gun and hotshot detective, huh?'

Pat grinned rather than register resentment of the label. 'Somethin' like that, I guess. Whatever you might've heard about me, I'm denyin' every word of, though. Would you be willing to show me where this happened?'

'Not today, for danged sure. I said I wasn't noways scared to hang out up there in the dark alone once. I ain't makin' that brag no more. We could ride up there come first light, though.'

'It's almost supper time anyway,' Callie interrupted. She turned her attention to Pat. 'You'll be eating up at the house with us, won't you?'

Clyde gave a loud snort. 'Too highfalutin to eat with the crew, is he?'

With no expression of humor, Pat said, 'Now why would I eat with you and that ugly cat when I have the chance to eat with someone as beautiful as Callie?'

This time Callie only grinned at Clyde instead of blushing, waiting for another loud snort which she knew would instantly issue from him. She wasn't disappointed.

The supper was not in the least disappointing either, nor was the

Hebert family's company. He especially enjoyed the way Callie participated in every discussion. As the meal and the conversation that followed it wore on, it became more and more a conversation between himself and the one he had decided was the most beautiful woman God had ever set upon this earth. He wanted the evening to last forever. It was clear she was wishing the same when he tore himself away and headed for the bunkhouse.

12

Pat Harmon arranged his camp carefully. Away from the cliff, he spread out his bedroll and built a fire. He built it larger than normal. Like all true Westerners, he always built a fire small enough for it to fit in his hat, with carefully selected dry wood that wouldn't smoke during daylight. He placed it where it was shielded from all directions at night, so it wasn't clearly visible.

There were several reasons for that caution. A small fire was adequate to make coffee and cook a meal. More than that was without purpose and wasteful. The greater reason was knowing that the less visible he was, the less he invited unwanted visitors, whether human or animal. A fire of any size, or one not located in a hollow of ground, was visible for miles at night. He hadn't survived as long as he had by being foolish.

He also knew enough to put his bedroll where it couldn't be approached easily or quietly. Having a dog was a good defense against surprises in the night, but he still relied on his own ears and senses as well. He had always marveled at the stupidity of many of the rustlers, horse thieves, and bandits whom he had surprised in their beds as the sun came up. Many times he had been sitting on a stump, their guns already collected, his own gun trained on them as they fought off the haze of heavy sleep. Why men on the run would be so careless, he never understood. It had often made his job easier, but he marveled at it, nonetheless.

Perhaps that was the reason for the knot in his gut as he arranged this campsite. His bedroll was in the open, easily approachable from nearly any direction. The fire was on a low knoll, where it would be visible from ten miles away, once it got dark. Even the dying embers of the fire would be a clear beacon, signaling his presence to anyone who might be in the area. He deliberately selected a few pieces of greasewood that would smoke, so the smoke would be visible before it got dark. All in all, the campsite was nothing less than an advertisement blazoned across the mountain side that said, 'Here I am'.

On the gently sloping hillside, 200 yards below him was the campsite that Clyde Upton had pointed out to him. It was there that he and another hand had discovered the bodies of both Patrick O'Moynihan and his dog. They had been sent to search out the cowboy when he failed to return to the ranch. He and the dog had been dead four days when they were found, but the evidence of their violent death was still stunningly obvious.

Fifty yards behind Pat's campsite was the cliff. That was where the Hoover boys had wisely placed their own bedrolls when they were caught in the area as darkness fell. Pat had nodded and smiled with appreciation as he surveyed their choice. He had no doubt it was the only thing that had permitted their survival. On that greater slope, strewn with dry brush and sticks, it would be impossible for even a ghost dog to approach in silence. In addition, the curve of the cliff prevented attack from any direction except straight in from the front.

He fixed his supper and ate, all the while feeling the uneasiness of violating every rule of survival he had abided by for the years he had lived by his gun. He kept telling himself that any attack that came would come after dark, after the moon had set. Even so, the knot of uneasiness in the center of his stomach made it difficult to finish his meal. Dougly got a greater portion than normal as a result.

He sipped the last of his coffee as he watched the shadows lengthen and deepen across the mountainside. He listened to the normal night sounds as nocturnal animals, birds and insects began to stir. Another time he would have been filled with a deep sense of peace and well-being as he studied the idyllic scene and drank in the scents and sounds of the mountain. Tonight he felt only an increasing sense of dread.

He knew his adversary was physical. He was sure it had to be some sort of animal. He was not in the least superstitious. Even so, he well knew there were spiritual forces in the world that were very real. Every piece of evidence he had picked up in the area reinforced his conviction that the killer was physical, neither ghost nor demon. Even so, Sunka Wanagi continually popped into his mind — the Lakota words for Ghost Dog. He hadn't heard the term before, and he realized a very large number of folks in the area were convinced that it was real, and that it was responsible for the killings.

Every time the term sprang into his mind, he felt the hair rise on the back of his neck. Now, camped in such a way as to invite its attention — whatever 'it' was — the feeling was worse. It was two hours short of midnight when the moon settled out of sight and deep darkness stole away even the differing shades of shadows. In the gloom Pat stuffed branches of sagebrush he had gathered into his blankets to resemble the shape of a sleeping man. He stood his boots beside the bedroll, and slipped on a pair of moccasins in their place.

'C'mon, Dougly,' he said softly.

He and the dog moved as quietly as possible back away from the campsite. He sat down with his back against the cliff, in the deepest recess he had spotted. From it he could clearly see the embers of the campfire he hadn't doused. His rifle, resting on his knees, was fully loaded and cocked. He held the pistol grip, his finger on the trigger guard, one swift flick away from the trigger itself. Dougly lay beside him, head erect, sensing his master's tension, watching and listening with eyes and ears far better than the man's. Pat was as ready as he could be. He just wasn't at all sure what he was ready for.

The stars moved slowly and silently, as minutes wore away into the silence of hours. The moon had been gone for more than three hours when the first sound reached the dog's ears. He stirred slightly, his head lifting. A barely audible growl rumbled in his throat. Pat laid a hand on the dog. 'Easy, Dougly,' he breathed softly. 'Stay.'

A couple minutes later he heard it as well. Something moved in the darkness. Dougly's hackles stood straight up. Pat could feel, with his hand on the dog, the low rumble of a growl, which the dog didn't allow to become audible. He jumped nearly to his feet moments later when the scream of a mountain lion ripped through the night. He understood as he never had before, why animals that knew movement would be fatal could not remain still when that sound shattered the night around them. It was all he could do to remain seated against the face of the cliff.

Without his hand to steady him, he

was certain the dog wouldn't have remained where he was. Even with that reassuring hand, the dog trembled. The softest of whines escaped in spite of his best efforts at silence. Listening intently, Pat thought he could actually hear the cougar's footsteps. He told himself it was his imagination. Even so, he heard something. He was sure of it.

Was the killer nothing more than a rogue mountain lion? He dismissed the idea as quickly as it rose in his mind. No mountain lion simply kills and leaves. True, a lion that finds a number of easy victims, such as calves or colts or sheep in a corral, will kill a dozen or more of them for the sheer delight of the kill. But even then, they would eat at least part of their kill. Whatever was killing in this area killed only people, save the one attack on the cowboy's dog, and never ate so much as a bite. The cougar that stalked him now was almost certainly not his quarry.

Tiny sounds impossible to identify broke the stillness of the night. Pat strained to hear, to discern the direction of the sounds. His finger moved to the trigger of his rifle. He sat with every muscle tensed, straining, willing his eyes to penetrate the inky blackness they could not pierce.

Loud noises erupted without warning. At first he thought it was the lion again. But it wasn't a normal roar. It was the strangest sound he had ever heard from a catamount. It was followed with the crashing of brush, as if the night concealed some pitched battle. It was not a normal battle, however. Any battle of carnivorous animals he had ever witnessed was accompanied by a cacophony of growls, snarls, yaps, howls and yelps. This battle was totally silent except for the noise of brush and ground being smashed and ripped apart. With his mind screaming at him to remain silent, Pat's fear overrode his intellect. He held his rifle where it was across his knees and fired three times rapidly into the darkness. He had no hope of hitting anything in the darkness. He just couldn't resist the urge of his survival instinct to shoot at whatever threatened him.

It was over in scant minutes. The echoes of his wild shots died down. Deathly silence settled over the mountainside once again. Pat felt his hands tremble as he pointed his rifle this way and that, awaiting a rush of motion he knew must come any moment. He continued to wait until his hands began to ache. He released the forestock of the rifle and reached a hand down to the dog. To his surprise, Dougly's hackles were no longer lifted. His head lay on his front paws. He appeared to be watching and listening, but with no sense of alarm.

Pat frowned. Why wasn't the dog afraid any more? Why was he signaling that there was no imminent danger? What did his ears and nose tell him that Pat had no way to discern? Eventually he decided to trust the dog. He lowered the rifle's hammer carefully, knowing he still needed only to thumb the hammer back and squeeze the trigger to fire it. He leaned back against the rock wall of the cliff, aware for the first time how tense his muscles were. His back and shoulders ached. His hands had lost the tremor their fatigue had created, but they felt stiff and tired. He leaned his head back, feeling the brim of his hat crush downward. He left it that way, letting the beaver skin of the Stetson cushion the stone.

Questions swirled in his mind. Did he dare sleep? What had happened out there in the dark? Was the lion still there, waiting? Why had nothing attacked his bed? What were the snarls and other sounds that didn't sound like a lion?

The dying embers of his campfire had long since faded to darkness. Nothing broke the black stillness but distant stars, that twinkled and winked at him, but shed no light on the earth or on his questions. Sometime he dozed off. He hadn't intended to. His hand lay on the back of the dog lying beside him. He knew the faithful animal would sense danger long before he would, and would alert him. Even so, he intended to stay awake and alert.

He didn't. He woke with a start, realizing that the first rays of dawn already streaked the eastern sky. His eye darted to his horse. The big gelding grazed contentedly on the patch of grass against the cliff that his picket rope permitted him to reach. He looked at his bedroll, with its pretense of a sleeping man. Nothing seemed to have been disturbed.

As light slowly began to seep into all the cracks and crevices of the mountain side, he peered intently all around. Nothing seemed out of place, abnormal, or strange. It was as if the strange and eerie noises of the night had been some weird dream. When the sun had fully extinguished the night lights of the stars, he moved the hand forward that still rested on the dog's back. He scratched behind his ears, and was rewarded by the silent wagging of the animal's tail. He rose to his feet. He pumped his legs up and down, stamping out the stiffness from muscles and joints. He gathered a few sticks and rebuilt the fire. He shook some Arbuckle out of its bag into a small kettle of water, and set it in the coals at the edge of the fire. As he waited for it to boil into coffee, he picked the branches of sage out of his blankets and shook the blankets free of stickers and brambles. By the time he had it tightly rolled and tied, the coffee was just rising to a boil.

He moved it from the fire and tossed a splash of cold water onto it to settle the grounds. He waited half a minute, then poured some of the steaming black liquid into a cup. He cupped the mug with both hands and continued to study the country around him through the steam of the hot brew he carefully sipped.

Half an hour later, his hunger sated with a couple dried biscuits and some jerky, with his second cup of coffee warm in his stomach, he picked up his rifle and set out with Dougly to scout the area for tracks. He walked unerringly to the source of the last of the eerie sounds that had assailed him in the darkness. When he had almost reached the spot he thought they must have originated from, Dougly emitted a low growl. At almost the same time Pat spotted the tawny hide lying prone in the brush. Rifle at the ready, he approached slowly.

One of the biggest mountain lions Pat had ever seen lay stretched out on the ground. The area around it was torn up from some colossal battle. Brush was smashed and broken. The ground was gouged and clumped. Grass was strewn about. Blood was everywhere, as if some geyser of blood had been turned around and around, spraying everything in reach.

He stepped over to the lion, then stopped in stunned surprise. There were almost no marks on the animal, except for the throat. The throat of the beast had been completely ripped out. Pat could picture the image of the terrified and furious animal whirling around and around, trying to reach its attacker, all the while its great heart feeding that geyser of blood that painted the area.

Had the lion attacked something that then killed it? Had it been the prey, rather than the attacker? What creature existed that could possibly do that to a mountain lion, and live? Pat shuddered in spite of his best efforts. He experienced an instant's urge to get on his horse and ride out of the country. He didn't owe anybody in this country a thing. He didn't hardly know anyone here. If he had a brain in his head he would ride away and let them deal with whatever was out there by themselves.

Even as the thought crossed his mind, the image of Callie Hebert hovered enticingly there. If he left, he would never have the chance to get to know her better. He had never met a woman he was so instantly attracted to as he was to her. Not only that, but if he left, whatever was out there might very well pick her as one of its victims. The thought of her meeting the fate of the lion at his feet was overwhelmingly intolerable. He muttered a reprimand at Dougly, who was licking at the lion's blood, and began to walk a circle around the dead animal.

The ground was dry and hard. The area around the puma was too torn up to yield any clear sign. He had worked an ever-widening circle until he was nearly a hundred yards from the dead animal before he found the first sign that had any value to him. He squatted on his heels and studied it closely. It was a single track. He frowned at it, as if it were somehow offending him. 'Looks like a dog, or a wolf,' he said quietly to Dougly. 'Way too big for a coyote. Too big for a wolf, for that matter. Too big for any dog. Big as a bear track, but it sure ain't like any bear track. Wrong shape completely. What is this thing?'

Dougly offered no explanations. 'Follow it, Dougly,' he commanded.

147

The dog sniffed the track, then began to walk the direction the track was leading. His nose was close to the ground. His tail was down, almost completely between his legs. He made it perfectly clear that he had no desire to follow whatever it was, but he obeyed. He led Pat nearly a quarter of a mile before Pat was able to see any more sign. Across a small space of moist ground beside a seep spring, he found tracks. 'There's two of 'em!' he exclaimed. 'Whatever it is, there's a pair of 'em.'

He studied the tracks for a long while. 'Sure look more like dog tracks than anything else I've ever seen,' he said at last. 'But if they're dogs, they're the biggest dogs I've ever heard of.'

Dougly followed their trail for another eighth of a mile, until the pair entered a stream. They had evidently followed the stream, walking in the water one direction or the other, for a ways. He couldn't find where they emerged on either bank. At last he returned to his horse and headed out. All he had to show for a terrifying night was more questions. Maybe someone at the LRH could shed some light on the mystery. If not, at least he'd have a chance to visit with Callie for a while.

13

Pat glanced at the sky. Less than an hour left before sundown. He turned his horse back toward the way he had come.

It was late. It was far too late. He was already two hours too late realizing the time. He had intended to search for tracks of whatever animals had killed the mountain lion until mid-afternoon. That would give him plenty of time to get back to the LRH ranch before dark. Suddenly a dark tide of fear welled up within him, making his heart pound at the same time as a shiver ran down his back.

He couldn't ever remember being afraid before. Ever. He had found himself in situations that he well knew might end his life. Scant weeks ago he had stood in the dusty street facing Red Atkins, fully knowing the man might well be quicker than he with a gun. If so, he would die. So be it. He felt no fear.

He had walked, guns blazing, into a hive of hired guns, to eliminate the cause of a town's subservience. He had heard the whine of angry bullets past his ears, felt them tugging at his clothes, and been temporarily deafened by the deadly voices of those guns. Through it he had known that the next instant might well be his last. Indeed, he well knew it would be a miracle if he walked out of that place alive. But he had felt no fear. He returned fire swiftly, cooly, methodically, and he had emerged unscathed. Even in reflecting on it afterward, there had been no icy stab of fear. Fear was simply something he had never felt.

He had tracked killers and rustlers and outlaws and Indians. He had stood toe to toe with the ruthless and the seemingly unbeatable. He had long since come to terms with his own mortality and knew he wasn't going to live for ever. There had been many days he knew the odds were overwhelming that he would not survive to see the sun go down. But he had never felt real fear. It simply was not in him to feel fear.

Now, for the first time in his life, he was afraid. For the first time he felt the rising tide of terror that had sent better men than him screaming from the battlefield, or reduced them to blubbering masses of humanity huddled helplessly on the ground. Whatever killed that lion, he was afraid of. It was just as simple as that. He would not spend another night out alone in the area of death in which that formless monstrosity reigned if he could help it.

But he had been so intent on finding where that pair of animals emerged from that stream he had lost track of time. What was more, he still hadn't found what he sought. It was as if they had stepped into the rushing waters and been dissolved. First downstream, then back upstream, he followed slowly along both banks. Neither he nor

Dougly could find a trace of the phantom creatures again. They killed a full-grown mountain lion, apparently with ridiculous ease. They walked away, with no evidence of any rush. They entered the creek. They never came out.

Now he was at least five hours away from the LRH, and less than two hours from darkness. The way back to the ranch lay directly through what he had come to think of as the cordon of death. It was in that one area where all the deaths of which he was aware had occurred. It would be pitch dark when he rode through it.

The moon set an hour earlier every night. There would be moonlight for a little while, but even that would be slim. It had been a waning moon that offered little light last night. It would offer less tonight. He lifted the big gelding to a swift trot. He'd best cover as much ground as possible while he had the daylight. The lower the sun sank toward the mountains, the greater his discomfort grew.

There are times, it seems, when some premonition creeps over us, portending things that are about to happen. We aren't supposed to have that kind of sixth sense. We suspect that animals possess something of it, watching their unease at the approach of a storm, but how they know escapes us. Even so, we feel it sometimes. Some vague uneasiness in the core of our being sends out signals of alarm that we sense, but fail to understand. Maybe it was the fear and encroaching darkness that triggered the feelings in Pat. Maybe it was his fear that telegraphed itself to his faithful horse, that caused its unease. Maybe the horse, in turn, transmitted that apprehension to his dog. He could clearly see, from the way his dog trotted with his tail between his legs and his ears laid back, that he was far from comfortable. Maybe all that fear being transmitted and relayed was simply feeding on itself, and they really had nothing to fear. Maybe.

On the other hand, maybe the

remnants of some primeval instinct still linger in our beings, surging up in times of peril. Whatever the case, there was one thing of which Pat Harmon was certain. The farther he rode, the more uneasy he became. The same phenomenon was painfully obvious in both his horse and his dog.

The sun slid down behind the mountain tips, taking one last peek at the land then disappearing, as if it, too, found wisdom in flight. Fingers of darkness deepened in shadowed places, then reached out broadening hands to conceal more and more of the surroundings. From within those shadowed and murky places occasional movement rocketed Pat's hand to his gun. Twice the impulse drew the weapon before the phantom movement melted away, and he holstered the Colt, feeling embarrassed. Once he looked around, hoping no one saw.

The sliver of moon provided enough light for him to keep his horse at that ground-eating trot, until the cowardly yellow moon followed the sun into hiding. As deep darkness settled across the land, he slowed the horse to a walk. Stridently though his inner voices screamed at him to hurry, he well knew a fall, or a horse's broken leg, would be a far greater danger than fleeing slowly. Once, as he passed through the area of his greatest fear, he distinctly heard a noise, somewhere in the darkness to his left. Both horse and dog heard it as well. Dougly woofed softly, as if wanting to provide only a quiet and furtive warning. The horse merely swivelled his head, his ears pointing momentarily in that direction.

Pat reined in and sat still in the saddle for a long moment, listening. He heard nothing more. Neither animal gave any further notice. He shrugged and surrendered to the clamoring nerves that urged him to resume his flight.

Two hours later the sound that reached them was unmistakable. Faint at first, then growing steadily stronger and louder, the sound of a running horse approached them from the rear.

Straining his eyes in the darkness, Pat reined his horse into a darker shadow and turned to face whatever approached. He didn't remember drawing the pistol that was in his hand. He could dimly see Dougly, lying down right at the horse's front feet, staring fixedly toward the approaching sound. 'That's either a wild horse in full flight, or somebody that wants his horse to bust a leg,' Pat told himself. 'Or somebody runnin' from the devil himself.'

As if in answer, the phrase, 'or one of his demons,' sprang into his mind.

The thundering hoofs of the horse were within a hundred yards when the sound abruptly changed to the crash of the horse as it fell, and the separate crash of a rider that was sprawled onto the ground. One short squeal of a human voice was the only other sound. He had no idea how he identified that one brief sound. The instant he heard it, Pat had no doubt who and what the sound indicated.

Without any thought of what he was

doing, he called out, 'Callie!' as he leaped from the saddle and sprinted in the darkness toward the sound he had heard. As he ran, some part of his mind noted that the horse clambered to its feet, snorting and blowing, prancing in fear, then moving away. 'Go get 'im, Dougly,' he told his dog, probing the darkness frantically for some sign of the horse's rider.

'Callie!' he called again. 'Is that you?'

This time a soft moan responded to him. It came from almost at his feet. He dropped to his knees and began to feel, able to see only vaguely in the dim starlight. After a few moments of frantic groping, he felt cloth, then the softness of flesh within it. 'Is that you, Callie?' he asked again.

Relief flooded through him when a voice responded with a breathless slur, 'Pat?'

'Yeah. Yeah, it's me. Are you OK? Where do you hurt? What happened? What in the name of thunder are you doin' out here alone in the middle of the night?'

In answer she only groaned as she sat up. With him gripping her arms, she struggled to her feet. 'I'm . . . I'm OK, I think. Tony must have tripped on something.'

'What was you runnin' from?'

The question brought memory flooding back past the daze of her fall. Her sharp intake of breath made a sound somewhere between a wheeze and a squeal. She grabbed Pat, clinging frantically to him. 'Pat! It's after me! It's chasing me! Tony outran it, I think. He's really, really fast. But it's coming.'

He put an arm around her, hugging her to himself protectively as he pointed his gun in the direction from which she had come. He could see nothing, hear nothing, sense nothing. Then, from the other direction, something stepped on a dry brush, crackling it in the dead stillness of the night. He whirled, still holding Callie close against him, to face whatever approached. Relief washed over him as he recognized the measured tread of a horse walking. In moments he could make out the movement of Dougly, one rein in his mouth, leading Callie's horse.

'It's all right, sweetheart,' he said, totally unaware of the term of affection he had just used, 'it's Dougly. He's got your horse.'

She made no move to push away from him. The term, however, was not lost on her. She looked up into his face, vainly trying to see him in the darkness. 'He got my horse? He's holding the rein in his mouth and leading Tony? How did he know to do that?'

'I sent him after it, when he got up and started off.'

'He can do that?'

'For you, I 'spect he could do just about anything. I could anyway.'

Instead of responding to the words he couldn't believe he was hearing himself say, she suddenly remembered the reason for her headlong flight. She whipped her head around, looking

160

again at the direction from which she had come. 'Is it still . . . ?'

He holstered his gun. 'I don't think so.' He answered her unfinished question. 'Neither Dougly nor your horse seem to sense anything out there, anyway.'

Still without taking his arm from around her, he turned his head. He gave a short, sharp whistle. She jumped at the unexpected sound, then simply leaned more closely against him as she realized what it was. Almost at once he heard, then dimly saw, his horse walking toward him, head held to one side to avoid stepping on the trailing reins. 'We'd best get movin', though,' he said. The reluctance was evident in his voice, even as the fear he had been fighting all night was beginning to rise within him again.

She was more open with her feelings. 'I don't want to move,' she said. 'I just want to stand here, feeling perfectly safe because you've got your arm around me.'

He didn't need to be told twice to keep his arm there. 'What are you doin' out here in the middle o' the night anyway?' he asked again.

'Do I have to be honest?'

'Absolutely.'

She sighed, then looked up at him in the darkness. 'I was riding out in hopes of meeting you. I thought I just might meet you on your way back to the ranch before dark, and we could ride back together. When I didn't find you, I just kept riding and looking for you. I didn't realize how late it was getting until it started getting dark. Then I was so afraid! I started for home, and I was . . . oh, I don't even know. Back there somewhere. And I felt something. I couldn't see anything, but I felt something was there. Tony felt it, too. Or maybe he heard something. Anyway, his ears went back flat against his head, and he started snorting. He never acts like that. I was so scared! I just knew it was that ghost dog, or whatever it is. Did you find it? Did you learn anything about it? Why are you so late coming back? Tony really wanted to run, and I did too. I just kicked him and yelled at him to run, and he did. Oh, Pat, he can run so fast. I've raced him a few times. Did you know that? He's beaten everybody's fastest horses in the country. When he started running, I was sure I heard something behind us. He heard it too, and even when he was running what I thought was his fastest, he started running even faster. I couldn't see a thing, it was so dark, and I just knew he was going to trip on something and fall and I'd be killed or that thing would jump on me and rip my throat out and . . . Oh, Pat! I was so scared!'

She dissolved in tears, the salty torrent finally halting the rush of words pouring forth from her. She flung both arms around him and gripped him as if hugging him hard enough would crowd the fear from her. Pat wrapped his own arms around her, intensely aware of the feeling of her body pressed against him. Part of his mind watched his dog for any indication of her pursuers. Most of him just wanted to wrap his whole being around her and draw her into himself for all the rest of his days. He lowered his head, smelling the freshness of her hair that flowed out from beneath her hat. As she tipped her head back, he felt the chin cord that held that hat on brush the side of his face. Then their lips met. If the ghost dog had appeared at that moment neither of them would have noticed.

It was a long time, and no time at all, until she stepped back, putting both hands gently on his chest. 'We have to get home,' she said, her voice sounding strained.

'I reckon,' he grudgingly agreed. 'Your folks gotta be worried some by now.'

'Father is going to be furious with me,' she agreed. 'I didn't even ask him if I could ride up this way.'

'Why not?'

'Because he'd have forbidden it.'

'And would you have come anyway?'

She was suddenly glad for the darkness that hid the rush of blood to her face. Her voice was soft as she said simply, 'Yes.'

'So you didn't ask permission.'

The darkness also hid the impish grin, but he heard it in her voice anyway. 'Sometimes it's a lot easier to get Father's forgiveness than his permission.'

'How 'bout one more kiss before we go?'

She hesitated, then stepped up and gave him a quick kiss that wasn't nearly what he was hoping for. Then they were both in the saddle, riding slowly and carefully, chatting as if they had known each other for years instead of the couple weeks since they had met. They were less than a mile from the ranch when they met the whole crew, riding out in search of them. Home had never looked so good to Callie. Pat felt only a sense of disappointment that they were there.

14

'Patty O'Moynihan rode for me once. I don't take it kindly when someone or something kills one of my hands, or them as I know. I don't care how you do it, but I want you to find out what it was. If you can kill it, or him, or whatever it is, so much the better. But find out.'

Walter Finney scowled at Vincent. 'He'll not be finding anything of this earth, Clay. I'm telling you, there's a demon been set loose somehow, and the only way we'll see an end to the terrors he wreaks is if this wicked country turns from its evil ways in repentance. It's an emissary of Satan himself, I tell you, and the only force strong enough to combat it is the spirit of the Lord. The wickedness of this evil generation is reaping its just reward.'

'Patty was a good man,' Clay Vincent

retorted. 'If it was God's justice it'd be you that was the target, for the way you treat your hands and cheat 'em outa their wages.'

Pat fought down the urge to ask Finney how a man as fanatically religious as he seemed to be would have, at the same time, such a strong predilection for booze as he had been demonstrating over the past couple hours. Instead, he said, 'I have a real problem thinking it was anything supernatural.'

'And why is that?' Finney demanded.

'Well, as I heard it, the Hoover boys blasting holes in the dark with their rifles apparently scared it off, after their dog tangled with it. I doubt a demon or a ghost or anything supernatural would be affected by bullets.'

'Their bullets drew no blood,' Finney argued. 'The boys both said they found no blood.'

'Bullets don't usually draw blood blasting holes in the air,' Pat observed. 'The point is, they scared it off.'

'Or it simply chose to withdraw in

demonic glee to torment them another time,' Finney rejoined. 'Or maybe it recognized them as two innocent boys and not among the wicked upon whom the good Lord has allowed the devil to loose his minion.'

'So your point is that this thing only attacks the wicked?'

'Of course. It's clearly and obviously an instrument of Satan that God has allowed to harass and destroy the doers of iniquity.'

'Doesn't that make you uneasy?'

'Why would it disturb me?' Walt Finney shrugged. 'I am a righteous man, and I live in fervent fear of the Lord.'

Pat couldn't resist the opportunity to needle the self-righteous zealot. 'Isn't drunkenness one of the things the Good Book calls sin?'

The jab didn't faze Finney in the least. 'It is for a fact, and I am thankful that I am not among that lot. I do imbibe, as the Lord Himself was known to do and was called a winebibber for it. But I am not a drunkard. I can enjoy a nip on occasion, or I can do without whenever I so choose. I could stop drinking entirely at any time if I felt it to be called for.'

Clay snorted, nearly choking on the beer he had just taken a drink of. 'Yeah, sure you could, Walt. Just like old Whooshtay can mop up the saloon without finishing off every swallow left in anyone's glass.'

'That's not the point at all, boys,' Oscar Osbeck interrupted the increasingly heated exchange. 'The point is, if it ain't something supernatural, what is it?'

'It has to be supernatural. It's sure not an animal, anyway,' Silas McGovern interjected. 'At least, not any animal I've ever heard of. An animal that can kill like that, kills for food. I've never heard of one that kills, then doesn't even try to eat any of what it killed. And this thing doesn't kill other animals. Nobody's lost a single calf to it, so far as I know. Or a horse. Not even a colt. Nothing has been attacked except people. And no person could rip out a throat that way.'

'Of course it's neither human nor animal. It's a demon, I keep telling you,' Finney insisted. 'It is sent to attack the sinful. Nothing else makes any sense. If there is not a general and widespread repentance, we shall all die.'

'I think old Whooshtay's right. It's 'Sunka Wanagi', the ghost dog.'

Clay snorted again. 'Walt's demon makes more sense than that.'

Half a dozen of the area ranchers and homesteaders had met in the saloon in Prosper Gulch at Pat's request. He thought it would be a better use of time than riding from place to place, visiting with each one separately. So far, he had learned exactly nothing that he didn't already know.

His attention kept straying from the pointless bickering among those in attendance. More and more he was determined to keep his headquarters at the LRH ranch, and work from there to try to solve the mystery. It seemed to be the ranch closest to the location of most of the killings, and the place where one of the only survivors of an attack could be found. Besides, that was where Callie was.

He was brought back to the present by a harsh voice from the bar. 'Hey, cowboy! Is your name Lyle Young?'

It took a moment for Pat to realize the speaker was addressing him. When he did, he simply shook his head. 'Nope. Never heard the name.'

He turned back to the group assembled at the back corner of the saloon, but the voice interrupted again. 'You sure look like him.'

Pat turned his attention back away from the speaker and started to address the group, but the speaker was having none of it. He strode purposefully across the room and stopped, his legs spread slightly, and pointed at Pat. 'You are,' he declared with conviction. 'You're Lyle Young.'

'Who's Lyle Young?' Walt Finney asked.

The speaker pointed a finger at Pat.

'Him, that's who Lyle Young is. But I don't blame him for denying it. I'd deny it too, if I'd done what this man did.'

Alarm bells went off in Pat's mind as he recognized he was being deliberately targeted for some reason. Maybe the man was honestly mistaken. It seemed more likely that he was deliberately looking for a fight. He stood up, stepped clear of his chair, and addressed the speaker. 'Who are you?'

'Don't matter none who I am. What matters is who you are, and what you're doin' in these parts. Things get too hot for you down around Laredo?'

'I've never been to Laredo in my life.'

The man laughed harshly, one short 'Hah! Now I know better'n that. Now that I got a clear look at you, I know danged well who you are. You're Lyle Young, the guy that shot that homesteader with the good-looking wife in the back, then raped and killed her as well. I bet you didn't think anyone would recognize you clear up here, did you?'

Pat's mind raced. The charge was ludicrous, but how would anyone know if it were true or false? Given time, he could easily prove he had never been near Laredo, but that provided no solution to the instant loss of his credibility if he allowed the charges to go unchallenged.

His voice flat and hard, Pat took a step toward the speaker. His eyes bored holes into those that taunted him. 'Mister, I'll give you the benefit of an honest mistake, if you're makin' one. You can back off and admit you're mistaken.'

'Oh, I ain't mistaken,' the speaker assured him. 'I'd know you anywhere, Lyle Young.'

'Well, then, you are a liar. I don't know what your game is, but you've got three choices,' Pat said. 'You can turn around and hightail it outa that door before I deal with you for lying about me, or you can take your best swing before I beat the truth outa you, or you can go for that gun that looks like it's seen a lot of use. Who hired you to get rid of me and why?'

The gathered group noticed for the first time that the man indeed wore a very well-used forty-five, tied low on his hip. His hand was inches from it. It was instantly apparent to every one of them that his purpose in the charges he made was to provide himself an excuse for his real intent. That reason, it was suddenly clear, was to kill Pat Harmon.

More swiftly than any of them could follow, the speaker's hand arced upward with his forty-five. As it neared to level, Pat's own pistol roared. The would-be assassin grunted and took a step backward. A second shot from Pat's gun followed so swiftly it sounded more like an extension of the first report. The gunman staggered backward a step, then crumpled to the floor. His gun, unfired, lay in the sawdust inches from his limp hand.

Pat stepped forward and kicked the gun farther from its owner's hand. He watched the gunman carefully for a long moment, assuring himself he was dead.

When he was convinced the man was dead, he thumbed the spent brass from the cylinder of his Colt and replaced them with fresh shells. Then he holstered the gun. He turned back to the group. 'Anybody know who he is?'

To a man, they all shook their heads. Pat turned toward the bartender. 'Do you know him?'

The bartender shook his head as well. 'He's been showin' up once in a while over the last six months. Once a month, maybe. Never talks to anyone. Never has offered his name. Has a drink or two, listens to folks talk for a while, usually spends a little time upstairs with Ida Lee, and leaves. She's the dark-haired gal over at the end of the bar, if you want to talk with her.'

Pat walked over to Ida Lee. 'You know that man?'

She looked at the dead man sprawled on the floor, then back at Pat, clearly rattled. She took a deep breath. 'I need a drink.'

Pat turned to the bartender. 'Bring

the lady a drink. Not tea this time.'

The bartender nodded and poured a shot of blended bourbon from a bottle beneath the bar into a shot glass and slid it across the bar to Ida Lee. She took the glass and tossed its contents off neatly. As she wiped her mouth with the back of her hand, Pat said, 'I take it you knew him?'

Ida Lee nodded. 'I knew him. Not well.'

She was visibly upset at the man's death, but was either unwilling or unable to offer anything of substance. 'He's been sort of one of my regulars, for, oh, the last six months or so. He was pretty close-mouthed, though, even when he'd been drinking.'

'He tell you what he was doing in the area? Who he worked for? Whether he had a homestead someplace?'

She shook her head. 'Like I said, he never said hardly anything. He wasn't rough, like some guys. Just seemed . . . normal, but awful quiet. That was all right with me.'

'He didn't talk about himself at all?'

'No. He just did what he came for, got dressed, and left, till the next time he came to town.'

'You don't have any idea where he came from?'

'Maybe from Dakota Territory, but I can't really think of anything he actually said that made me think so.'

'Did he ever mention bein' in Laredo?'

'No, I'm sure he never mentioned Laredo.'

'I figured as much. Is there anything else you can tell me?'

She shrugged. 'Not really. Oh, well, maybe. One thing. He always paid real good, but he paid in gold.'

'Gold? Gold eagles?'

She shook her head. 'No. Gold. Just plain gold. He always had a little bag of it in his pocket. I always had to take it to the bank and they weighed it and exchanged it for money. But it was always more than what I charge. He never tried to cheat me.'

Pat frowned, trying to make sense of

that revelation, but it made no sense, so he dismissed it. He turned back to the bartender, and tossed some money on the bar. 'Pour Ida Lee another drink. She could use it.'

'Thanks, mister,' she said as she eagerly reached for the shot glass and waited for the bartender to refill it.

Pat returned to the group. 'Well, that was a big blank. Other than the fact that he hadn't ever mentioned Laredo, I don't know any more than I did.'

'Well, he had you targeted, for a fact,' Oscar Osbeck observed.

Heads nodded around the table. 'Which probably means he heard enough to know you men had sent for me to solve the killings,' Pat offered.

'You think he wanted to kill you to keep you from it?' McGovern asked.

'That'd be my guess,' Pat confirmed, 'which would seem to argue against the idea that we're up against something supernatural.'

Nobody could offer any argument with that logic.

Pat rode out of town at first light. He convinced himself that he would travel around the country where the killings had taken place, seeking clues. He was certain he wasn't going to camp overnight in that area. He was equally sure he would find himself at the LRH within a day or two. He really had a great deal of difficulty thinking about anything except Callie Hebert.

15

Sometimes the best intentions simply slip away almost unnoticed. Plans made don't always take into account the vagaries of human emotions. In the end, it is those emotions that dictate a great many of our actions.

Pat Harmon had every intention of exploring carefully the region surrounding where the long list of victims of the 'ghost dog' had been killed. When he rode out of Prosper Gulch, he would have insisted that that was where he was heading. In fact, as if of its own mind, his horse beat a steady and straight path directly to the LRH ranch.

Pat wasn't aware of having changed his plans. He wasn't surprised at arriving there. It was as though his intention all the time had been to return there upon leaving town.

His arrival was hardly unexpected,

either. He wasn't into the yard yet when Callie burst out the door of the house, heading toward him on a dead run. Only if she had been watching for his arrival could she have spotted him that quickly.

As she approached, Pat stepped from the saddle. He was surprised at the fervor with which she launched herself into his arms, and of the ardor of the kisses with which she greeted him. He was not in any way put off by it. Just surprised. It was uncommon for a young lady to demonstrate that level of affection so openly. Still, he couldn't think of a reason in the world to object.

He did notice the tight lips of her father as they approached the house, an arm around each other's waist. His first words were, 'Harmon, you and me need to have a talk.'

He stepped off the porch and strode directly away from the house, his back to them. Callie looked up into Pat's face, apprehension suddenly replacing the joy that had radiated from her face since first spotting his approach.

'Looks like you'd best go on into the house,' he told her. 'I'll be in shortly.'

Callie looked back and forth between Pat and the retreating back of her father twice. She planted a quick kiss on his lips and walked toward the house, turning her head back around several times before she disappeared into the front door.

He dropped the reins of his horse and walked to where Lester Hebert stood waiting, well out of earshot of anyone in the house or yard.

As Pat approached, Lester said, 'Harmon, my daughter seems to have quite a case for you.'

Pat nodded. 'It sure ain't one-sided, Les. I ain't never felt for a woman what I feel for Callie.'

'You been takin' advantage of her?'

'Not a bit. We ain't got nothin' to hide. She's a fine woman, and I wouldn't do anything to hurt her reputation for the world.'

'So what are your intentions?'

Pat hesitated a long while. Then he said, 'Well, I got a little bit of money saved up. Till I came here, I wasn't sure what I was savin' it for. Now I can't think of ever doin' anything that doesn't include her. I've thought some of bein' a lawman, but that ain't much of a life for a woman and kids. I guess what I've been thinkin' of the most is puttin' together a small herd of cows and start buildin' a ranch.'

'You got that kinda money saved up?'

'Nope. Enough to get started, but not in a big way for sure. But if we each homestead on adjoining claims along Thistle Crick, we could range stuff up into the mountains in the summer. There's some nice hay meadows that'd let us put up feed for winter. It'd be a nice spot to live, and close enough she wouldn't have to be too far away from you and Ruth.'

'Sounds like you've been puttin' a lot of thought into it.'

Pat scratched the back of his neck self-consciously. 'Yeah, I'm afraid I have. Truth be known, I'm afraid I've been spendin' more thought on that than what I've been hired to do.'

'So what are you doin' about that?'

'To be real honest, I ain't much closer to figurin' it out than I was when I got here. What happened in town last night sure convinced me it ain't no ghost dog, though.'

'What happened?'

Pat briefly filled him in on the confrontation in the saloon.

Les digested the information, lips pursed, his brow knit down hard between his eyes. 'That don't seem to go together none.'

'It does if there's someone behind the killings, that's doing it to scare people away. Keeping the legend of the ghost dog alive would add to the spookiness of it, and make folks more afraid.'

'Yeah, I'll allow as how that could be, but it leaves a couple awful big questions. Three, would be more like it. Number one, who would do somethin' like that, just to scare folks? Number two, if there was someone like that, how would they manage to do what they've done? And number three, what could anybody gain by doin' it?'

Pat smiled ruefully. 'Well, that only leaves me three little details to get figured out.'

Les nodded. 'Not to mention tryin' to keep your own throat connected to the rest of you while you're doin' it.'

'Yeah, I'd sorta like to do that, too.'

'You dang well better do that part of it. If you go gettin' yourself killed after my little girl's done fell head over heels for you, I'll put a bullet in your dead carcass just for good measure.'

Pat grinned. 'Does that mean I have your permission to court Callie?'

Les snorted. 'As if you need my permission. Seems to me that's already gone past what I'm likely to have any say about. But for what it's worth, you got it. Just don't go hurtin' her, or runnin' off and leavin' her. If you was to do that, I'd find you. And if I couldn't, I 'spect Clyde could. And would.'

Pat nodded. 'I sorta noticed those two were awful close.'

Les nodded in turn. 'Clyde's been like a second pa to her since she was born. He'd lay down his life in a second for her, if he had to.'

'So would I,' Pat replied. 'So would I.'

Les brought the discussion back to the reason for Pat's presence there. 'So what's your plan now?'

Pat shoved his hat to the back of his head and scratched his forehead. 'Well, I was wantin' to get you and Clyde and Callie around the table and draw me a map of the whole area. Canyons, gullies, ridges, bogs, beaver dams, caves, springs, cricks, anything of any importance in the lay of the land. Then we can mark where each of the killings happened, as close as we can, and see if it makes any sense.'

Les nodded. 'That'll likely have to wait till after supper.'

He turned and strode back toward the house, with Pat keeping pace. As they neared the house, a hand appeared as if from nowhere. 'I'll take care of your horse if you want, Pat.'

Surprised, Pat looked the young cowboy over. 'OK. Sure. Thanks.'

'No problem,' the young man replied as he picked up the gelding's reins and headed toward the barn.

As he and Les stepped up onto the porch, Callie came out the door. 'Well?' she demanded.

'Well what?' Les replied in his gruffest voice.

'Well, does my knight in shining armor have my father's permission to court me?'

Les snorted. 'Now what makes you think we was even talkin' about you?'

'I know you, Father. I saw the way you scowled like a gargoyle when I kissed Pat.'

'I didn't notice you askin' my permission for that.'

Callie giggled. 'Are you going to give me permission to do it again? You better hurry if you are, because I'm about to do just that.'

Without waiting for his response she flung her arms around Pat's neck and planted a kiss on his more than agreeable lips. Les snorted yet again and went on into the house, trying his best to act offended and angry.

Callie kept her hands locked behind Pat's neck. Her eyes danced as she stared into his. 'Well, did you ask my father's permission?'

Pat's eyes twinkled in easy likeness of hers. 'Well, he gave me permission to paddle your behind if you don't do as you're told.'

Her eyes opened wide in mock anger and surprise. 'If you think you can do that, you just try it, big man. You may learn a thing or two about me you'd do well to remember.'

'Is that so?'

'Yes, that's so. So did he give you permission?'

He found himself totally unable to keep up the charade. He grew suddenly serious. 'As a matter of fact he did, Darling Callie, and I told him that if you'll have me, he'll be stuck with me being his son-in-law just as soon as I can talk you into the idea.'

The fervor of her kiss provided him all the answer he needed.

16

Stuffed with delicious food, followed by strong coffee, Pat wanted nothing more than to find a quiet spot where he and Callie could snuggle up together and begin to plan their future. As with most things in life, however, there were other things that had to be dealt with first.

When the table was cleared, Lester brought out a piece of paper and a pencil. He quickly sketched out the primary features of the area. The sketch showed the nearer mountains, the creeks, the major canyons, the timbered areas, and whatever came quickly to mind. Comments from Clyde added to the details and accuracy.

Pat nodded as he watched the two dimensional picture of the area come into existence. He recognized enough of the features from his riding the area to confirm its accuracy.

'OK,' he said, when it appeared the map was as complete as it was likely to get, 'let's put an X on each spot where somebody's been killed.'

Lester marked the spot of the homesteader's body, the couple from the wagon train, Patrick O'Moynihan, and the others whose deaths were identified as part of the plague of death that had the area terrified.

'How about the Hoover boys?' Pat asked.

'Their camp was right here. Same spot as where Patty was killed.'

'How about where you ran into it?' he asked Clyde.

'Same spot.'

'Right busy patch of ground,' Pat observed. He stared at the map for several minutes. Then he pointed to a crooked line that started in the near mountains and stopped not too far from Thistle Creek. 'What's this?'

'That's Rattlesnake Canyon.'

'Nice friendly name. Sounds like a perfect spot for a picnic.'

Lester chuckled drily. 'It is now. There used to be about the biggest rattlesnake den I ever saw right about here.'

As he said it, he placed a finger on a spot about halfway from the mouth of the canyon.

'Used to be?'

'Yeah. We got tired of havin' so many cows and horses gettin' snake-bit up around there. We waited till the country was froze up enough to have 'em all in the den, then we went up there and planted pertneart a case o' dynamite in it and blew it to kingdom come.'

'Blew up half the danged mountain is what we did,' Clyde observed.

'You managed to get all the snakes?'

'Oh, probably not all, but there couldn'ta been too many left. There was snakes and pieces o' snakes flyin' all over. We found and killed all those we could find that wasn't dead yet. There was prob'ly some we missed, but all told I'm guessin' we killed a thousand snakes.'

Pat whistled. 'Wow! That's a lot of rattlers.'

'Saved a whole lot o' livestock, anyway. We ain't had much of a problem with snake bites in the two years since.'

'That was just two years ago?'

'Yup. Up to then we didn't know where the den was. We knew there had to be a big one, what with so many rattlers in that area. We just hadn't found it.'

Callie chimed in for the first time. 'We probably wouldn't have found it then if it hadn't been for the baron, or whatever he was. That canyon is pretty narrow and steep and rocky and all that stuff. Stock never did stray up that way, so we didn't have any call to ever go that far up into it.'

Pat's eyes rose quizzically. 'Baron?'

Lester nodded. 'Some sort of European nobleman, I guess. Him and his dogs found it.'

Pat frowned, struggling to make sense of the revelation. 'What was a European baron with dogs doing in this country?'

'Tryin' to find somethin' he wasn't already bored with,' Clyde muttered.

Callie grinned. 'Clyde didn't like him, in case you didn't notice that in his tone of voice.'

Clyde snorted. 'Anybody that hunts with dogs, just to watch the dogs kill stuff that don't need killed, then just rides off and leave it layin', ain't fit to be in the country.'

'He hunted with dogs?'

Callie offered the explanation. 'He had some really big dogs. Irish wolf-hounds, or something, he called them. They were as big as small horses. They could chase down deer, or even elk. He would give them a command to chase something, and they'd chase it down and kill it. He'd grin and watch, then he'd just leave it there. He didn't want the meat or anything. He just wanted to see if his dogs could kill anything that ran wild in this country. They killed deer and elk and at least one black bear that I know of.'

'Really! I didn't know any dog could kill a bear.'

Callie responded, 'I don't think just

one of them could, but they worked in pairs, or sometimes threes. They were really good at what they did. It was just senseless killing, though. When people figured out what he was doing, the whole country turned against him.'

'What happened to him?'

Lester offered the only answer that seemed available. 'Nobody knows, really. He had hired a couple drifters that was workin' as guides, showin' 'im where there was whatever kind o' game he was wantin' his dogs to tear up. Like Callie says, folks didn't cotton to what he was doin'. I guess he got tired of being shunned and such, and left the country. I always sorta figured him and his guides prob-ably headed up higher in the mountains somewhere to see if his dogs could kill a grizzly. He'd mentioned that a time or two.'

'But he's the one that found the rattlesnake den?'

'Yup. His dogs was chasin' somethin' up that canyon, and he run onto a lot of rattlers right close to one spot. He kept his dogs away from 'em, and watched 'em till he saw several of 'em crawl into a hole in the side of the canyon. He got close enough to figure out it was a small cave that went back quite a ways.'

'And he told you where it was?'

Lester nodded. 'That's how we found it.'

'How did you manage to get the dynamite in far enough to do more than just cave in the entrance?'

Clyde offered the explanation. 'We waited till she was down around about twenty below. When she's that cold, snakes can't move. In the den they just all get together in a great big ball. They ain't plumb numb, 'cause it ain't that cold in a cave or a hole in the ground. But they're all huddled together, and about half asleep or somethin', so you can shove a box o' dynamite right up close to 'em and crawl back out backward.'

'It'd take somebody braver than me to crawl in there,' Pat asserted.

Both Lester and Callie glanced

quickly at Clyde, but he gave no indication of even having heard the statement. It was instantly clear to Pat who it was that had dared to do so.

Lester broke the awkward silence. 'We strung out a fuse long enough so we was sure none of them sidewinders was gonna get wrapped around our necks when we blowed it up. We set 'er off, and boy, howdy, did we get a show!'

Clyde chuckled. 'We mighta used just a wee mite too much dynamite.'

Lester agreed. 'We mighta used three times too much dynamite. We blew what started out as a small cave into a big crater in the side of the mountain.'

'Artillery shells in the war didn't make holes that big,' Clyde agreed.

Pat studied the map on the paper again. 'Wouldn't that canyon be just about in the middle of where some-body's been killed?'

Three pairs of eyes jerked to the map as if drawn by a single string. Callie's eyes instantly jumped back up to lock on Pat's eyes. Both Lester and Clyde continued to stare at the map. Finally Lester said, 'Not right in the middle, but not far from it.'

'Close enough for something from that canyon to reach all those places in two or three hours, though,' Pat offered.

After another long moment of looking at the map, Lester said, 'Yeah, easy enough. Do you think whatever it is lives in that canyon?'

Pat frowned at the map a long while before answering. Then, 'Well, it seems like that might be something worth taking a look at, anyway.'

Callie's face gave ample evidence that she had no desire for him to do so. Pat wondered fleetingly whether some woman's intuition prompted her obvious fright. He shrugged off the premonition. What had to be done, had to be done. Even if it meant his own death in the mouth of some ghost dog he still refused to believe in.

17

The bay mare was a pretty good horse, but it wasn't his own. The big gelding that belonged to Pat needed a rest. Accordingly, Lester had made several of the ranch horses available to him to use as needed.

Normally, a cowboy needed at least six horses in his own string. They worked the animals they rode pretty hard, from sunup to sundown. They covered long distances, lunging up hills and sliding down talus slopes. They went from a leisurely trot to a hard run instantly when commanded to do so, then slid to a halt when the rider's rope settled over the head of a critter that needed some sort of attention. Then they held the rope taut while the rider doctored, disentangled, or checked on that cow or calf or steer. Then they set out in search of whatever else needed tending to.

Following a normal day of work, a horse needed at least a couple days' rest. If a horse came up lame, it needed an even longer rest. During roundup, branding, weaning, etc., it was common for a cowboy to change horses at noon. A full day of intense activity simply exhausted the strongest of horses. Mares were also bred regularly, to produce continuing stock for the remuda. When they were heavy with foal or nursing, they could do little or no work. Consequently, every hand needed several horses to carry the load of the work demanded of them. The care they lavished on those horses reflected their importance to them and to their work. A cowboy without a horse was nothing. If he ended up without a horse a long way from home, he might well be a dead man.

If the ranch hired a cowboy that owned only the horse he was riding, the ranch made the spread's remuda available to him. From it, he would pick the horses that would be part of his string. Nobody else on the ranch would ride those horses. As long as the cowboy worked for that ranch, those horses were as much his as if he owned them, and he cared for them accordingly.

Pat, riding in from other areas, did not have such a string of his own. As was the custom, Lester made the remuda available to him, as if Pat had hired on as a cowhand. The mare he now rode was part of that string.

He rode out of the ranch yard fully two hours before daylight. From the pattern of the killings, he was confident that whatever was doing them would be en route back to its lair by then. That gave him at least a couple extra hours of daylight before prudence dictated he be back at the ranch.

He was a little frustrated that the mare didn't cover the country like his big gelding. She was a good horse and had a smooth gait, but the gelding had spoiled him. His long stride just covered a lot more ground than most horses. At the end of a day, it made a big difference in distance traveled.

The mouth of Rattlesnake Canyon spread out and flattened a hundred yards from Thistle Creek. As he waded the mare across the swift stream and rode into the broad confines of the canyon, he felt the hair rise on the back of his neck. He glanced at Dougly, trotting along beside the mare.

The dog gave no indication of any uneasiness. He panted happily as if on some great adventure. He snuffled the occasional trail of some bird or animal that crossed their path, then ran to catch up again. He seemed not to have a care in the world.

'Must just be my nerves,' Pat dismissed the feeling.

Rocks and gravel kept the center of the canyon almost free of vegetation. Swift water, coursing down from the mountain side, had carried tons of rocks and debris along with it for centuries. Most of it ended up in the middle of the canyon. That formed a wide swath that contained no vegetation.

Almost at the edges of that wide path of rocks, the sides of the canyon began their ascent to the ridges that comprised both of its boundaries. Near the mouth of the canyon, he was able to ride on the grass, beside the rocks and gravel. By the time he was a mile up the canyon, that was no longer possible. The sides of the canyon became steadily higher. The bottom, except for that deep bed of rocks and gravel in the center, was more and more choked with brush. It was too thick, and the sides too steep, to allow passage of man and horse.

It was necessary then to allow the mare to pick her way carefully over that unstable path, where almost every step caused a rock to roll or move from under her hoof. It was slow going. The rocks that turned and rolled seemed to make an uncommon amount of noise. It seemed to Pat as if the sides were closing in on him, trapping him, suffocating him, hemming him in from both sides.

Dougly seemed to increasingly share his sense of apprehension as they advanced. He began to move with his tail down. There was no more of the happy sense of adventure in his posture. Instead of panting happily along, he moved almost stealthily, his nose up, testing the breeze that rippled down the canyon. From time to time his hackles rose, then flattened again.

Watching the dog served only to heighten Pat's own sense of imminent danger. He glanced up at the sky, trying to gauge the position of the sun. He could only guess at it. The sides of the canyon cast the entire breadth of it into shadow. Later in the day the sun's rays would reach the canyon's bottom for a brief time, but now it lay in continual gloom.

A cottontail rabbit burst from a bramble patch, ducked and dodged along the rocks, then dived into another thick patch of brush. The mare twitched and tossed her head at the unexpected noise and motion, but did not shy. Dougly scarcely gave the normally tempting rabbit a glance. That worried Pat as much as anything. If Dougly ignored a rabbit, there was some scent on the wind that he deemed of far greater importance. For a moment he wished for the dog's sense of smell.

A rock rolled under the mare's foot, causing her to stumble. She caught her balance at once, and Pat was no more than rocked momentarily in the saddle. The thought ran through his mind that his gelding would not have allowed that to happen. Even as the thought rose, he recognized that even that sure-footed animal would be hard pressed not to stumble on the difficult path he was asking of the mare. It did little to lighten his mood.

Against his will, a scene from another time and place played across his memory. He had been riding up a gully much like this one, but neither as deep nor as long. A friend rode beside him. Both wore badges, and were following the trail of the one remaining fugitive from a stage holdup. With no warning, his friend grunted. Simultaneous with his fall from the saddle, the sound of a rifle shot echoed down that gully.

Pat had dived from his horse just in time to avoid a second shot from the hidden assassin. He had no way to know if his friend was dead or only wounded. If he tried to help him before dealing with the shooter, he would more than likely be shot himself. He really had no choice but to deal with that threat first.

He called to his friend quietly twice, but received no answer. He moved swiftly to the edge of the gully, then scrambled with the furtive silence of a woodland creature through 300 yards of brush to a position from which he could see the assailant. He shot him before the man was even aware of his presence, exactly as he had killed Pat's friend. That was the only killing he had ever been called upon to do that really bothered him. He assured himself that the man was a killer. He needed to die. He would be hanged if Pat brought him in as a prisoner. He would have killed Pat if he had spotted him. Even so, it went against his nature to shoot the man without at least giving him the opportunity to surrender.

When he had returned to his downed friend, he was dead. Even though it was clear he had died instantly from a bullet to the heart, Pat felt guilty for leaving him long enough to deal with his killer. That sense of guilt rose in him again. Guilt for leaving his friend for that brief time. Guilt for killing their assailant without warning. Guilt for feeling guilty about doing what he had to do.

Emotions can play strange tricks on our senses. Lost in his struggle with those old feelings, he almost missed the flash of sunlight on a rifle barrel high on the side of the canyon.

Instinct, finely honed from a dozen near-death encounters, made his body react even before his conscious mind knew why. He dived from the mare, landing in a thick tangle of plum bushes even as the sound of a rifle shot reached him. Ignoring the tears in his clothing and skin from the thorny branches, he crawled several feet to the twisted trunk of a Russian olive tree and stood up behind it. He peered carefully around the tree, suddenly aware that his rifle was in his hands. He couldn't remember jerking it from the saddle scabbard as he dived from the horse, but his instincts had taken care of that detail as well.

As he studied the far side of the canyon, he saw a small puff of smoke. At almost the same time his mare grunted and toppled over sideways.

Cursing under his breath, he jerked the rifle to his shoulder and fired three swift shots at the spot where he had seen the puff of smoke. There was neither response, nor any return fire. He looked around, trying to spot his dog. He was nowhere to be seen. Sudden fear lurched up into his throat. He swallowed hard. He called softly,

'Dougly. C'mere, boy.'

In seconds that seemed like hours the dog emerged from the thick brush almost at his feet, crawling on his belly but unhurt. 'Good boy,' Pat said with relief.

He studied the spot from which the rifle had barked its message of sudden death. He could see nothing out of place.

He looked at the mare, lying flat in a pool of her own blood. His lips drew to a thin line as fire flashed in his eyes. He wanted, more than anything in the world, to start up along the steep side of the canyon, find the shooter, and do to him as he had tried to do to Pat, and as he had done to the innocent mare.

Stark fear kept a rein on the urge. Whoever had shot at him must surely be tied in with whatever was doing all the killing. Whatever or whoever he was, he had control over something that most people were convinced was other-worldly. Whether ghost, demon, or some exotic and formidable living creature, he had to admit he was afraid.

He realized with a sudden chill that his horse had been killed for a purpose. He was now afoot, near the lair of that unknown and vicious something that killed with such fierce and terrible ease. He had just been tagged as the creature's next victim, just as certainly as death itself.

He swallowed hard, trying to control the sudden pounding of his heart. Crouching low, he went to the prone mare and grabbed his canteen, slinging its strap over his shoulder. From a saddlebag he grabbed two handfuls of rifle shells and stuffed them in his pockets.

'C'mon, dog,' he said softly. 'Let's find some sunshine.'

As rapidly as possible, he began to scale the side of the canyon, moving through the thick brush with as little noise as possible. He gave no thought to staying out of sight of the hidden rifleman's position. He was inexplicably certain the man was no longer there.

He was absolutely sure he had gone to fetch whatever agent of death it was that he kept at his disposal.

It took Pat and the dog over half an hour to scramble upward to the top of the canyon's rim. Once there, he swivelled around, prone on the ground, and studied the canyon. There was little to see. The whole of it was so choked with trees and brush that he all he could see was the tops of branches. From where he lay, the rocky trail along the bottom was totally invisible.

He turned and looked over his shoulder. He was more than a dozen miles from the LRH ranch. He was afoot. The only thing going for him was that it was still daylight. Whatever it was that was surely already summoned to seek him did not normally operate in daylight. He might have a chance, if he could cover enough ground before the darkness overtook him.

At the same time, he well knew the difficulty of walking that far in riding boots. Their high, underslung heels were made for stirrups, not strolls. The pointed toes were designed to find the off stirrup quickly when mounting an unruly horse. He had never walked more than a mile wearing boots. Even at that lesser distance, he'd ended up lame, walking slowly, and too distracted by the pain in feet and legs to remain alert to pursuit.

He slid backward from the rim of the canyon. When he felt safe in doing so, he stood and stretched the kinks out of his back. 'Well, dog, we'd just as well get started,' he told the faithful canine.

Even as he began the walk in long strides that he knew would soon shorten, a nagging voice in the back of his mind insisted that he and his dog would die together without ever laying eyes on the LRH again. Or Callie.

As he thought of Callie, saw her face before him, felt her body pressed against him, tasted her lips against his, he swore softly that he would use every ounce of strength and cunning he owned to make it back to her. Even as he made the vow, he knew his chances were someplace between slim and none.

18

It was back there. Or they were back there. Either way, death dogged his trail. He knew it, even without the soft whines from Dougly when each errant breeze brought some scent only his nose could identify. The dog merely confirmed the feeling. It was there, biding its time, keeping pace, awaiting the darkness.

Pat tried to pick up his pace. He stumbled and nearly fell. Pain enveloped both feet, radiated up his legs and shot fire through his hip joints. It sent sharp messengers upward, driving spears of agony into the small of his back at each step. He clenched his teeth against it, willing himself to keep walking.

The doe that broke from cover and bounded away over the top of a hill did not merit a glance. The jay that scolded from the top branches of a tree received no notice. He was dimly aware of the half dozen buzzards that circled high above him, but he refused to acknowledge their presence. He kept his eyes fixed on the direction of his walk with dogged determination.

That was why he spotted the motion before Dougly did. Nearly a mile away, he caught just a glimpse of movement as something or someone topped a ridge and dipped immediately back down below the skyline. He had less than a second's glimpse, but he was sure it was a horseman. Hope surged upward in him. A rider, riding openly, would certainly not be the thing that pursued.

He managed to pick up the pace of his walk, but only momentarily. Within a hundred yards, he was back to the woodenly determined swinging of one foot in front of the other. He saw nothing of the rider he was sure he had spotted.

Half an hour later he approached a finger of timber jutting out into the long grass-covered slope he was ascending. His path would take him twenty yards from the tip of the timber. Beyond it the whole long slope would be open to his gaze.

As he walked, his gaze swept back and forth, more from habit than by conscious thought. As his glance passed the tip of the trees he froze. He jerked his rifle up, then lowered it with an overwhelming sense of relief. 'You been hittin' the bottle?' a familiar voice queried. 'I seen barflies that didn't stagger that much.'

Pat grinned through the pain that enveloped the lower half of his body in fire. 'No, I just been hittin' the ground way too many times with these boots. I could use a drink, though, if you just happened to have a bottle.'

Clyde chuckled for the first time Pat could remember. 'Where's the mare?'

'Dead.'

'How?'

'Shot.'

'That so? Whereabouts?'

'Rattlesnake Canyon. 'Bout three or four miles up from the mouth.'

'See who shot her?'

'Nope. Caught a flash of sun on his gun barrel and took a dive into a plum bush. He missed me. Then he just deliberately shot the mare. I put a couple or three shots at the smoke puff, but it ain't likely I hit him.'

'Thought maybe you'd best walk outa there, huh?'

'Seemed like a good idea at the time. I figured it must be whoever controls whatever's doin' all the killin'. I figured he shot the horse so it could track me down and get rid of me.'

'Reckon it's followin' you?'

'I'm sure of it. Hangin' back, waitin' for dark, most likely. Dog's been catchin' wind of it on a regular basis, he acts like.'

Clyde was silent a long moment. Then he nodded. 'Likely right. Well, Barney here's good an' stout. I 'spect he can handle us ridin' double. We got a couple hours o' daylight left. Maybe we can cheat the Grim Reaper one more time.'

'You showin' up sure helped the odds, anyway. How'd you come to be here?'

'Just lookin' after myself. That danged girl you seem to have corralled let me know in no uncertain terms that if I didn't get out here and back whatever dang-fool play you left in the dead of night to try to pull off, then I'd best let that critter have my throat too. Whatever it is, I'd rather face it than that Callie girl when she's upset. Now quit your jawin' and climb up here. Sweetie Pie, you git down.'

To Pat's amazement, the ugly tom cat perched on Clyde's bedroll leaped to the ground. Pat swung aboard and squirmed himself into as comfortable a spot as he could between the bedroll and the cantle. It wasn't the best, but it sure felt good to get off his feet.

It felt even better when Callie flew into his arms when he climbed down in the yard of the LRH ranch.

19

Pat was wide awake instantly. Even in the soft moonlight that filtered through the grimy bunkhouse window, he recognized Clyde.

'What's up?'

'Danged girl's already gone.'

He shot bolt upright in his bunk. 'Callie? Gone? Where?'

Instead of answering, Clyde growled, 'I shoulda knowed better. When we was layin' out our plans, and you told her she couldn't come, she didn't put up near enough fuss. I shoulda knowed she'd just jump the gun and get an hour's head start on us, so we couldn't catch her till we're too far to send her back.'

Pat bailed out of bed. 'What time is it?' he demanded as he hurried into his clothes.

'Still wants two hours of daylight. I

figger she's got a good hour's head start on us.'

'She'll head for that deer trail you talked about.'

The night before, gathered around the kitchen table, Pat, Clyde, Lester, Callie and Ruth had discussed Pat's discovery and his brush with death. Clyde and Lester described the way into the canyon, up high, closer to the mountains. There was a well-defined deer trail that the baron had discovered leading to the canyon bottom. It was that trail the two of them had followed with the dynamite that ended the plague of rattlesnakes and made a great crater of what had been their den. They had decided to try to make it to that trail by mid-morning, ease quietly down it, and see if they could discover the lair of what they had come to call the ghost dog, for lack of any more definitive name.

Callie had instantly insisted on going along. She pointed out that she could outride and outshoot any cowboy on the ranch. She insisted she had no intention of allowing Pat, Clyde and her father to launch that quest without her. When they all flatly refused to consider her going along, she had yielded. Too quickly, and too readily, they now realized.

As Pat hurriedly rolled up his blankets, Clyde said, 'I got the night hawk saddlin' your gelding, along with Lester's and my horses. Ruth's already got some chuck in Lester's saddlebags for us. We oughta be past the big hogback by sunup.'

They were well past that landmark when the sun first shot its searching rays across the land in front of them. From a high point they studied the terrain ahead. 'No sign of her,' Pat lamented.

'She may be tryin' to get clear to the canyon ahead of us,' Lester observed. 'She is one headstrong little filly.'

'Downright bull-headed, you mean,' Clyde growled.

'What's she ridin'?'

'That big sorrel Tennessee Walker.'

'That's what I was afraid of. That horse can cover more ground in a day than any horse in the country.'

'Then let's get movin'. Ain't no sense sittin' here chinnin', whilst she gets farther on.'

In silent agreement the three nudged their horses back into the swift trot that they could maintain all day. They said little, each lost in his own thoughts.

20

A soft noise in the darkness brought a gasp of terror from Callie's throat. She stifled it, forcing herself to listen silently.

A great horned owl lifted off the ground, holding a rabbit in its talons. It was framed momentarily by the full moon as it winged its way to its nest to dine in leisure. A sigh of relief exploded from the young woman's mouth.

It was too early in the night to be out alone. Whatever terrorized the country might not yet be back in its own lair. But she well knew that her father, Clyde and Pat would be in the saddle within another hour. She had no intention of being close enough to the ranch when they caught up with her to be sent back.

After all, she was neither a child nor a tenderfoot. She had been born and raised in the rough and ready life of the west, and was a match for whatever the raw land held. If she could, she would find that deer trail, sneak down it, and discover the ghost dog's lair before the men arrived. Then she would proudly point it out to them, then remind them of who had solved the mystery. She would probably remind them again at opportune times for months or years to come.

The light of the full moon made it easy for the walker to keep the rhythm of his swinging gait at a pace few horses could match. Being a walker, he moved both left feet forward together, then both right ones, instead of the left front with the right rear, and right front with the left rear as most horses did. That felt to the rider as if she were swinging back and forth sideways, but it allowed the horse to walk as fast as most horses could trot. In addition, it allowed him to walk at that speed all day without tiring.

She smiled as she shrugged down deeper into the coat collar turned up against the night's chill. By daylight she was three miles past the big hogback. Well before mid-morning she found the deer trail. She got off her horse and walked along it, studying the ground carefully as her father had taught her to do. She identified deer tracks, differentiating between bucks and does, and noting their relative sizes. She saw tracks of a bull elk, and what she thought might be a mountain lion track, but it was too vague for her to be sure. What she was most interested in was the fact that no horses or men had ridden this trail since the last rain. She could descend into the canyon in silence without worrying about someone lying in wait ahead of her. Once in the bottom of the canyon she would decide which direction to search. Perhaps she could find tracks there to help her quest.

Her horse made almost no noise as it followed the trail worn into the sloping side of the canyon. From time to time the trail would level off and follow along at the level, then veer downward again. Brush on all sides became steadily thicker. Twice her horse was barely able to scrape under overhanging branches. By the time she was halfway to the bottom she rode in deep gloom, beyond the reach of the sun's rays. With the fading light, her courage and her delight in being ahead of the men faded as well. A sense of impending doom nagged at the corners of her mind. By the time she reached the canyon's bottom, she was gripped by fear that threatened to send her scrambling back up that trail.

Only her pride prevented her doing so. She would not back down now! She was here first, and she would find the lair of that thing, whatever it was. She was not some silly parlor ornament to stand around giggling and gossiping. She would prove her mettle once and for all this day.

Still dismounted, she led her horse upward along the dim bottom of the canyon. It was almost totally covered with rocks and gravel in the center, and

226

all but impassable everywhere else. She followed along it for nearly half a mile before she found a wider spot where mud and silt had covered the rocks. There she crisscrossed back and forth half a dozen times, searching for any tracks that would help her quest. She found only the normal animal tracks that might be expected there.

She turned around and went back the other way. As she passed the trail she had descended on, she considered climbing back to the top. Surely the others couldn't be far behind by now? It would make sense to wait for them.

She clamped her lips and lifted her chin. No! She had no need to wait for anyone. She placated her fear by lifting her rifle from the saddle scabbard and levering a shell into the barrel. Holding it loosely in her right hand, the hammer cocked, her horse's reins in her left, she began to walk down the canyon.

She had gone scarcely a quarter of a mile when she rounded a bend and stopped dead in her tracks. She jerked backward, pulling her horse with her. She hurriedly tied the reins to the trunk of a small tree, then crept back forward carefully and silently.

As she reached a spot allowing her to see around the canyon's bend again, she surveyed the area. The canyon widened for nearly 400 yards. Though still thickly covered with brush and trees, it was much less constricted. Against the far wall of the canyon, where the rays of the sun actually managed to reach, was a log cabin. It was more like a log shack than a cabin. It appeared to have been hastily built, and little maintained.

Next to it was a large enclosure made of hog-wire stretched around tall posts. It was over ten feet high. The top row of hog-wire was bent over toward the inside, as if to prevent something from climbing out. Inside the enclosure three animals were lying on the ground.

Callie's mouth dropped open. She stared, unable to take her eyes off the animals. She recognized them! She had marveled at them more than a year ago, awed at their size and prowess.

'The baron's wolfhounds!' she breathed. 'Those are the baron's dogs!'

She slid backward into the brush. Trying to be as quiet as possible, she moved forward, straining to see who or what else was there besides the dogs. Beyond the shack and the dog's enclosure was a large cavity in the side of the canyon. She knew instinctively it had to be the crater left by her father and Clyde when they blasted the rattlesnake den.

She stepped out of the trees and brush, determined to cross to where she could peer into the lone window on the shack. She was less than three feet from the trees when a voice behind her froze her in her tracks.

'Lookin' for somethin', lady?'

She whirled. She stared into the snaggle-toothed grin of the dirtiest man she had ever seen. His unkempt hair flared out in greasy strands from beneath the battered hat. His beard had not been combed, trimmed, or even washed in a very long time. He turned and spat a brown stream of tobacco juice at the ground, then grinned at her again.

'I don't get a whole lot o' company out here. Matter o' fact, I ain't never had no company as purty as you stop by. I think this here's gonna be one mighty fun day.'

Struggling to find her voice, Callie stammered, 'Who . . . who are you? Those are the baron's dogs. Where is the baron? Why do you have his dogs?'

The man's grin only widened. 'Ain't you the clever one! They ain't the baron's dogs no more, though. He don't have no need of 'em no more. They might be hell-hounds, but he didn't get to take 'em to hell with him.'

He cackled at his own wit, the sounds of the laughter grating painfully on Callie's ears. 'He's . . . he's dead?'

'Deader'n a doornail. Buried right over there, as a matter o' fact. Wouldn'ta bothered to bury 'im, but he got to stinkin' plumb awful.'

'What . . . what happened to him?'

'He got hisself killed.' The man grinned.

'How? Why?'

'You ask a lot of questions. That's all right. I ain't had no one to talk to since Whitey didn't come back from town. You don't happen to know what happened to him, do you?'

Certainty flooded through her mind that she knew exactly what happened, but Callie shook her head quickly. 'I don't even know who you mean.'

The man shrugged. 'Don't matter none. He most likely got hisself killed too. Always havin' to run off to town every month or so, to find hisself a woman and some whiskey. I told him that'd get him killed, but Whitey, he didn't never listen. If he'da just stuck around, he'da found out that a fine lookin' woman just showed up right here. You didn't happen to bring a bit o' whiskey with you, so's I can have both, did you?'

He cackled again at his own wittiness. He kept looking her up and down appraisingly, clearly anticipating the sport he intended to have, admiring the good fortune that had stumbled into his grasp.

Desperately trying to stall for time, Callie demanded, 'What are you doing here?'

He chuckled again. 'Well, now, pretty lady, since you ain't goin' nowheres, now that you found me, I'd just as well tell you. Me'n Whitey was guidin' that there baron fella around the country, watchin' his dogs chase down and kill pertnear everything we found for him. After while, he sorta got tired of it, I guess. Talked about goin' up higher in the mountains, maybe findin' a grizzly for 'em to try killin'. But he wanted to come up here and have a look-see at where that ranch fella blowed up the rattlesnake den first. We're the ones that found it, you know. Me'n an' Whitey an' him. Well, we come up here and had a look-see all right. Only what me and Whitey seen was somethin' a whole lot better'n even what the baron was payin' us. That dynamite exposed a finger vein o' gold. Nothin' real big, mind ya, but enough gold to keep me'n Whitey in women and whiskey the rest of our lives. So we got rid of the baron, and then we set about to make sure nobody else got to hangin' around close enough to get nosy, till we had time to dig out that vein o' gold.'

Realization dawned slowly in Callie's eyes. She almost forgot her fear in her excitement at learning, at last, the answer to so many questions. 'Then . . . then it's the dogs that have been killing people?'

The man's grin widened enough she could see the disgusting brown fluid pooled inside it. 'That there's my doin',' he boasted. 'Trained 'em good. I'm right good at trainin' dogs. Trained 'em to tear out peoples' throats, without eatin' none of 'em. Trained 'em to just kill people, not animals, unless an animal attacks them. Thataway, folks'd think it was that ghost dog the old stories talk about. It goes agin' their nature, but I trained 'em that way anyhow. It worked too! Folks been shyin' away from this neck o' the woods just fine.'

'You can't get away with this!'

'Now just who's gonna stop me, pretty lady?' He drew his pistol as he spoke, but let it hang at his side, content to let her know he would gladly shoot her if necessary. 'Now, how's about you just droppin' that there rifle, and you an' me can stroll over there to my cabin. I'll show you all that gold we done got dug outa the ground, then you can show me some things I'm gonna enjoy just as much as that gold.'

'I will not!'

He only grinned more. 'Oh, we kin do it right here, I reckon. First time, anyway. I got nothin' against takin' you right out here in front o' God an' everybody, 'cept there ain't no everybody, and I don't reckon God's gonna help you none.'

His grin faded to the wickedest leer Callie had ever seen. His eyes flashed with sudden passion. His words fairly sizzled with venom as he said, 'Now I'm done talkin'. Drop that rifle and start peelin' off them clothes!'

Acting more on fear and instinct than rational thought, Callie jerked the rifle up to hip level. She grasped the forestock with her left hand, even as her right hand squeezed the trigger. The rifle roared impossibly loud in the confines of the canyon.

The man jerked backward, dropping his pistol. His eyes widened in surprise, then anger. Blood spread from a hole in his right shoulder. Callie levered the rifle to insert a new shell into the chamber. The rifle jammed, leaving her unable to fire again.

As she struggled desperately with the weapon, the man realized she was unable to shoot again. Instead of trying to retrieve his pistol with his left hand, he lunged across the canyon. He grasped the door of the dogs' enclosure and whipped it open. He pointed at Callie and bellowed at the dogs. 'Sic 'em! Sic 'em! Git 'er! Kill 'er!'

Three dogs lunged through the gate, each striving to be the first to reach her, to rip her throat out, to earn their master's praise and appreciation, to revel in the taste of warm blood. Callie backed against the brush behind her, frantically jerking at the lever of her rifle. The offending shell freed at last and fell to the ground. She worked the lever again. This time the shell entered the chamber smoothly. The first dog was already in the air, silently leaping for her throat, jaws agape, teeth impossibly large and gleaming. The rifle barked, seeming to fire of its own accord. The dog grunted, but was carried into her by its momentum. Its weight drove her backward, sending her crashing down into the brush with the huge animal on top of her.

She fought to twist herself out from under the savage animal, knowing any instant the teeth of the others, even if she had managed to kill the one atop her, would be ripping at her throat. From somewhere beyond the roar of blood that pulsed wildly in her ears, she heard a barrage of shots. Silence followed, more oppressive than the roar of the volley of shots. Then the weight of the dog was jerked off of her. Hands grasped her, lifting her. She fought to maintain her grip on her rifle, determined to keep the evil fiend from disarming her.

Slowly she realized it was not he who gripped her arms, shouting at her. 'Callie! Callie! It's me! Are you all right?'

She whipped her head back and forth wildly. She spotted her father and Clyde. Clyde was bending over the body of the man whom she had wounded. Two of the dogs lay dead, besides the one that now lay beside her.

'It's over, Callie! It's all right. You're OK! Are you OK? You're all right, aren't you?'

Callie looked into Pat's eyes and instantly passed out. When she came to, all three men were huddled over her. 'Are you all right?' Pat demanded again. 'Are you hurt?'

She shook her head, and struggled to her feet. Words began to pour from her in a torrent. 'I . . . I'm OK.

You . . . you got here. Oh, Pat, I'm sorry. I was going to be so smart and find the ghost dog's lair before you did. And they killed the baron. They trained his dogs. It's the dogs, Pat. The wolfhounds. And the gold. There's gold in the shack. Enough so that we can have that ranch. And his partner was called Whitey, and I think he's the one you had to shoot in town. And — '

The torrent of her words was abruptly halted as Pat's lips plugged the path of their flow. She jerked slightly, then threw herself against him, responding avidly. He thought he just might see how long he could keep her silent that way. At least, it seemed like a good idea at the time.

THE END

We do hope that you have enjoyed reading this large print book.

Did you know that all of our titles are available for purchase?

We publish a wide range of high quality large print books including:
Romances, Mysteries, Classics
General Fiction
Non Fiction and Westerns

Special interest titles available in large print are:
The Little Oxford Dictionary
Music Book, Song Book
Hymn Book, Service Book

Also available from us courtesy of Oxford University Press:
Young Readers' Dictionary
(large print edition)
Young Readers' Thesaurus
(large print edition)

For further information or a free brochure, please contact us at:
Ulverscroft Large Print Books Ltd.,
The Green, Bradgate Road, Anstey,
Leicester, LE7 7FU, England.
Tel: (00 44) **0116 236 4325**
Fax: (00 44) **0116 234 0205**

OLD GUNS

Ross Morton

Sam Ransom, broadsided by the death of his old partner Abner, learns of a note left by the dead man — warning that the infamous Meak twins are after Ransom's life because of what happened at Bur Oak Springs over two decades ago. Ransom knows he must alert the rest of his gang, who were there at the time. His family is in jeopardy and their only hope of salvation is the gang's return to confront the Meak brothers . . .

THE COMANCHE'S REVENGE

D. M. Harrison

For over twelve years, Kit Bayfield believed his son was dead. Back then, Kit's two other sons had been unable to find Mitch. But now, an Indian claiming to be his son, and going by the Comanche name of Broke, confronts him. Kit reckons folks will find Broke's return difficult. Everyone should have helped search for the boy and now his son's face is full of hatred — the whole town, including his brothers, is on his payback list . . .